MOONLIGHT OVER THE CINQUE TERRE

HELEN ROW TOEWS

MOONLIGHT OVER THE CINQUE TERRE Copyright 2023 by
Helen Row Toews
All rights reserved.
This book, or any portion thereof, may not be reproduced or used in
any manner whatsoever without the express written permission of
the author, except for the use of brief quotations in a book review.
This book is a work of fiction and, except in the case of historical
fact, any resemblance to actual persons, living or dead, is purely
coincidental.

Printed in North America
First edition, 2023

Edited by Under Wraps Publishing
Cover by Miblart

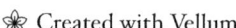 Created with Vellum

CHAPTER 1

"I'm sorry Tyler. But no, I can't marry you." Sarah lowered her gaze from his hopeful eyes, to where he knelt in a flowerbed, crushing a patch of her mother's pink petunias. It was the worst possible time for him to ask her, as it was just before she was to leave the country. Awkward too, since she'd asked Tyler to walk with her in order to break off their relationship for good this time. She stared down at the oversized grey sweatpants she wore and shoved her hands into the matching hoodie, her long blonde hair falling across her face. She would let him down gently.

As she took a breath to explain herself, he snapped open the lid of a small, blue velvet box and caught her wrist, endeavoring to thrust the case into her hand. "Just look at it." His eyes entreated her. "I picked out a diamond you'll love. Of course, it's smaller than I'd like, but someday, when I take over your family business..." He coughed, his cheeks reddening. "Anyway, it will mean a lot to me if you'd wear it."

Sarah took a step back and snatched her hand away. She could feel a headache brewing. Wait, Tyler planned on taking over her father's drilling company? When had that been discussed? He knew nothing about the oil business, always saying that working on the rigs her father owned was too dangerous.

Her parents liked her boyfriend, but for him to think he'd take over the company her father had spent his lifetime building, was presumptuous. Just like Tyler expecting she'd marry him after casually dating for a mere two months. She stared at him in shock.

"We don't have to set a date yet," he continued, jumping up to knock the dirt from his faded jeans. "Why don't you wear the ring as a promise? We can discuss dates...our future later when you get back from Italy."

"It's no good." Sarah protested. "I've told you several times I'm not ready for this. I won't agree to marry you or accept your ring." A sudden movement caused Sarah to glance toward the house where she caught sight of Jim. He was one of the gardeners who'd been with her parents since they bought the estate near Edmonton, Alberta. The man peered at them over a hedge he was trimming. Catching her eye, he ducked out of sight.

"How long do you need?" Tyler persisted, oblivious to all but his insistence that Sarah accept his proposal. "I love you, Sarah."

Sarah sighed. "Yes, you've been telling me that for a while now. But you won't consider the fact that I don't love you." She felt as though she were being harsh, but enough was enough. She didn't want to lead him on any longer and he wouldn't take no for an answer. "We've known one another almost two years now and dated for a few months, but even you have to admit we are more like friends than anything. We don't have what it takes to be married." She moved away from him and began walking toward the house. "You've got to stop this. Honestly Tyler, I don't think you love me as much as you imagine you do either," she muttered.

"I totally think we have what it takes," he stated irritably. "You just won't let me close enough to prove it." Disregarding her last statement, he increased his pace to stay abreast of her, shoving the ring box into the pocket of his jeans and irritably tucking in his white t-shirt.

She stole a sideways glance at him. Tyler was a good-looking man with a long, sandy-colored mop of hair that he kept out of his face with frequent flips of his head. He was tall, slim, and his shoulders were thrown back and erect as he strode beside her, his face looking like thunder. Usually his mischievous hazel eyes, a ready smile, and a quick wit made him fun to be with—but at the moment those attributes were replaced with a sullen frown.

Sarah stopped, exasperated. "How can you say that? The fact is, we don't have any chemistry and very little in common. We've been together almost every day and that hasn't changed."

"And whose fault is that? You kept me at arm's length the whole time we've gone out," he grumbled. "We weren't really dating, not in the physical sense." Tyler flushed angrily and fell silent.

"That's because it felt weird. We're only meant to be friends, Tyler. Please, let this go and move on. There's someone perfect out there for you if you'd just look," she waved an expansive arm and then pushed a tendril of hair away from her face. "It's really hot for June, isn't it?" It was a lame attempt to change the subject, but she was an optimist and smiled at him, praying he'd see reason.

She caught the distant sound of a jet and craned her neck to find the source. The sky was a rich blue with a single fluffy cloud to mar the perfection of the hot June afternoon. A thin, white contrail streaked across the cerulean sky, like a line of glowing smoke that stretched out to infinity. Sunlight glinted off the plane's silver edges. Sarah found herself wishing she were up there already and winging her way to Italy where she planned to spend the summer teaching English at a school in La Spezia.

But she wasn't. She looked at Tyler's red face as they marched across the expansive grounds. It was a beautiful place for an early morning walk. Sarah had enjoyed the trees, flowers, and many footpaths as a child. A fountain, squatting at the center of the manicured lawn, gurgled with bubbling water as they drew close.

Leaping ahead to come alongside the water feature ahead of her, Tyler grabbed Sarah's arm. "I can't believe you're doing this to me," he said, his voice hard. Catching her other arm, he pulled her around to face him. "You're leaving for the whole summer, and I thought you'd be wearing my ring. Can you promise you won't find someone else while you're away, and that you'll give our relationship some serious thought?" He pulled her resisting body into his arms. "I'm in love with you."

"I don't plan on meeting anyone else, but I refuse to promise anything...I already told you, we're breaking up," she said, curling her hands into tight fists. "You and I are friends. I really think you should start dating. Find a nice girl while I'm away." She laid a consoling hand on his sleeve. "Anyway, there are things I want to do before I get married. For one thing, I need to get a job and work for a while."

"Are you insinuating I don't earn enough money for you?" Sneering, he waved an arm at the manicured grounds surrounding them. "I guess you're used to better."

"No. Don't be ridiculous. Your job has nothing to do with it." She took a deep breath. "I just want to find my own place in the world. After all, I didn't spend four years at university for nothing." She smiled at him consolingly. "You'll be fine. Now, let's get back to the house. I have to finish packing. Dad's driving me to the airport later this morning."

"I could have..."

"No," Sarah interjected before he could finish. "My dad's driving me and we're picking up Gemma on the way." Under the circumstances, she didn't want to submit herself for yet another embrace. Hastily she put distance between them, almost jogging back to the house. Tyler doggedly followed behind.

"I'll text you when we arrive, okay?" she said, climbing the steps to the elaborate patio and trying to sound upbeat. "Think about dating, Tyler. I want you to be happy. Bye," She threw open the back door and waved.

"Yeah. Bye," Tyler shoved his hands deep into his

pockets and turned toward the driveway where he'd left his old pickup truck. Then, he turned back and shouted. "You think about what I said, too."

Sarah dashed inside the house breathing a sigh of relief. He'd been building up to this proposal for some time now, but she really didn't think he'd ask today. Maybe some time apart would help him to take stock of his life and realise this relationship wasn't what he wanted either.

Leaving for a couple of months was for the best. She'd just spent four long years in university to get her degree in education, paying her way through with summer jobs and tutoring on the side. Her parents agreed she should do something for herself before settling down to a full-time job teaching. So, when her best friend Gemma found the online advertisement, looking for people to teach English to adults for the summer, they'd both jumped at it. After having taken her only other holiday to France when she was nineteen, Sarah had always wanted to see Italy.

As she took the stairs two at a time to her bedroom, someone she'd met on that holiday floated into her mind, as he so often did. The memory of a man she had loved with all her heart—a darkly handsome Frenchman named Raphaël. But that was long ago, and she'd made a foolish, unalterable mistake, parting them forever. He was likely married with three kids by now.

CHAPTER 2

"Of course, you should have come with me!" Gemma's face registered the shock she felt. "I can't believe you're still debating it. Everything's booked. We're going to have a great time, too."

Angling her head, Sarah gazed out the train windows. They rode the Cinque Terre Express carrying visitors and villagers to and from the idyllic villages of the area. Flashing out of tunnels and into the dazzling sunlight of a late August morning, it offered only a brief glimpse of the wonders that were yet to be seen and enjoyed in this beautiful part of the Italian Riviera. The Ligurian Sea, off to Sarah's left, danced beneath an azure sky as tiny pastel houses, clinging to the rugged coastline, beckoned.

"It's not so much debating the trip. No, it's more feeling guilty for splurging on myself rather than grabbing the next flight home. I'm already sitting on the train to Vernazza with you, so I can't very well turn back now." Sarah shrugged. "I just need assurance that it wasn't too selfish of me to take another few days before returning to Canada. I should be looking for a job." She sighed heavily.

"You have to put work out of your mind. It'll take care of itself." Gemma placed both hands on her knees and leaned toward Sarah with grim determination on her face. "You worked all summer, remember. Teaching English to a bunch of Italian business people wasn't a picnic. I thought it was pretty demanding, didn't you?"

"Yes, but..." Sarah sounded worried, even to her own ears. "I don't ever want to sponge off my parents. Now that university's behind me, I need to get my own place and start earning a living."

"You will. Gimme a break." Gemma rolled her eyes. "You're about the most responsible person I've ever known. Too responsible if you ask me. You have to live sometimes, you know. We're only twenty-four! We should be having fun."

As the train plunged into another tunnel, Sarah averted her eyes to the blue-flowered skirt she wore. Brushing lint from her knee, she considered what Gemma said.

She took a deep breath and grinned across the aisle at her best friend. "You're right. I'll lighten up and have a little fun."

"And does Tyler still write you?" Gemma's face tightened a little with her last words. She hadn't been in favor of her two best friends dating and lost no opportunity in telling them so.

Sarah sighed. "Yeah, he texts." She didn't want to

discuss it. The subject had caused a few arguments between her and her friend. Sarah had only responded to Tyler's many texts once during the whole time she'd been away. And that was to tell him, yet again, to forget her and start living his life. She'd even told him she didn't want to be friends anymore. But from his messages after that, it didn't appear he was listening to anything she said.

Gemma sat back. Crossing her ankles, she put her hands behind her head as they emerged from another tunnel and turned her gaze toward the sea. She always dressed as though about to participate in a hiking expedition, and today was no exception. She wore longish khaki shorts, a pink tank top that bagged over her waistband, and clunky hiking boots with thick socks to protect her feet. Her customary ball cap had been pulled low over her eyes and large sunglasses completed the ensemble. A large backpack sat on the seat next to her and a cross-body purse, holding day to day items was slung at her side,

Gemma didn't fuss with makeup, preferring a fresh face. She left her dark brown eyes unadorned, although thick black lashes framed them nicely. Sometimes, she would smear a bit of clear gloss on her generous, smiling mouth. Though apart from that, she was as natural as she could be. Her hair was a glossy brown, the colour of roasted chestnuts, and fell to just above her shoulders. While her upturned nose was covered in freckles from all the time she spent outside.

"*Nessun problema*," she said, returning the grin once they were whisked into darkness once more. "See? I even learned some Italian while we were here. Anyway, that's what friends are for."

"What? For leading you on a wild getaway to the Cinque Terre?" Sarah laughed.

"Yes!" Gemma raised her voice with emphasis and then joined in the laughter.

Sarah's smile softened as they broke from the tunnel. She peered through the window once again. "It's so beautiful here. I want to enjoy every moment. Once I'm working full-time, and maybe married someday, who knows when I'll be able to return to this wonderful place? Maybe never. Even a working holiday was tough to swing on my budget." She watched as Gemma began to apply sunscreen to her face and arms.

"Understood," Gemma spoke soothingly. "I know you're fiercely independent and wouldn't accept help from your parents, even though they could easily have paid for anything you wanted. Still..." she added, "I don't think you should hurry home. We've been in Italy, yes, but we haven't seen much of it. We should make the most our chance to explore while we're here."

She paused and a hint of laughter entered her voice once more. "Maybe, when we end this trip in Rome, you could look up the Pope and ask for a holiday blessing. Then you wouldn't need to feel guilty anymore." Laughing, she dodged the brochure Sarah threw at her and dropped the sunscreen into her bag.

Sarah felt better. Over the last few weeks, she'd emailed her resume to as many schools back home as she could find. Only she hadn't heard from any of them, yet. Teaching jobs were hard to unearth and the competition was stiff. However, she had confidence something would turn up.

"So, tell me about this B&B you booked for us?" Sarah settled back in her seat as they flew into yet another passageway. "You said it's supposed to have gorgeous views, right."

"It does. The Cinque Terre is fabulous from every angle, or so I've heard." Gemma picked up the crumpled brochure and waved it in the air before tossing it back. "Weren't you reading about Vernazza? Our B&B overlooks the village and has a panoramic vista. You're going to love it." She looked smug.

"Did you take that line straight from the pamphlet?" Sarah grinned at her then spoke again, with gusto. "I know I'll love it." A round arch of light had appeared ahead of the carriage. A moment later they burst from the tunnel under the mountain and into the intense light of midday.

As the train ground to a halt, Sarah glanced at her phone to check for messages. It was a reflex action. She hadn't expected to hear from anyone today, since it was only about seven in the morning on a Saturday, back home. Here, it was almost three in the afternoon. They really shouldn't have slept in. Most of the day was already gone.

The journey had only taken about thirty minutes to get to Vernazza from their boarding house in La Spezia. Why hadn't she made this trip before? She slid the device into her purse and slung the strap of the voluminous sack over her head to settle it at her side, straightening with anticipation.

The train had stopped three times already, to

disgorge its passengers and take on more eager travellers. Gemma leapt up, following other passengers who rose to their feet and began shuffling toward the closest exit. Sarah waited for the throng of people to leave. Then, she reached into the overhead rack for her unwieldy bag, extended the handle, and dragged it down the aisle. She reached the steps, gingerly navigated them, jumped to the platform, and swung her bag behind her to skid across the cement.

Gemma waved to her over the heads of the many bodies all pushing for the exit and motioned that they would meet below the elevated station. She then set off, hoisting her backpack high on her shoulders, and tramping down the steps in her big boots.

Once on the street, Sarah spotted her friend at the edge of the rapidly dispersing crowd and made for her.

"First, we find the Azure Trail toward Corniglia," Gemma began in a loud imperious voice. "I think I see a sign for it over there." She pointed behind them to a high stone wall where an iron railing ran protectively along the top. At the spot where it joined the street there was a small plaque riveted to the rock.

"The B&B is a 600 metre walk. Up there," she waved a nonchalant arm toward the hillside as though it were just a quick jaunt around the block.

"What? Straight up?" Sarah almost gave herself a crick in her neck from looking up. She had expected a quaint little place in the middle of town, not some isolated dwelling suspended on the edge of an abyss.

It was pretty though. A jumble of colourful houses crouched along the lower portion of the mountainside, while rows of terraced vineyards ringed the rocky land almost to the top. The rollers of Sarah's case rumbled loudly across the pavement as she followed her friend toward the set of concrete stairs.

Sarah's heart sank. She could already see the foolishness of her attire, not to mention her luggage. Irritated with herself for lack of forethought, she now knew she shouldn't have worn a white blouse, flouncy skirt, and flimsy, high-heeled sandals. It was plain stupid. Of course, her friend could have given her a little warning.

As though knowing Sarah was thinking about her, Gemma shifted her backpack and stopped, turning to eye Sarah's hard-shell bag doubtfully. "Guess I should have told you it's all uphill and over rocky terrain." She made an apologetic face. "Oops."

"I'll manage. Thankfully, I only have to carry the thing up once. It's my own fault." Sarah fluttered a careless hand, denying her inner dread of the climb. "Let's go."

"Alright. Call me if you need help." Gemma swung around to stride away. She was shorter than Sarah's curvy 5'6" frame, but was lean and fit from her time spent at her favorite pastime—hiking. Gemma loved a challenge and positively glowed with the prospect of a good ramble.

Grimly, Sarah lugged her suitcase up the steps and started pulling it along the cement sidewalk. So far, so good. She eyed the rocky landscape ahead as the trail became increasingly steep. Squinting against the blazing sun, she watched as her friend turned the corner and disappeared. So much for calling her if she needed help.

Holding her suitcase between her knees to prevent it from rolling away, Sarah paused to dig in her handbag for a hair elastic, sunglasses, and folded sun hat. The hat wasn't the most attractive article of clothing she owned, but it worked. She scraped her long hair into a low ponytail, stuffed the hat on her head, and slid the glasses into place. Then, puffing a little already, she braced herself for the walk. Judging by where Gemma had gestured, it was almost straight up the hillside. She didn't mind exerting herself, but this was ridiculous.

Having forgotten to bring sunblock, a major *faux pas* in this country, she scrutinised her bare arms and wondered how soon they and her face would burn in the hot August sun. She should have asked to borrow some cream from Gemma. But the girl was already too far ahead to call to, having broken into a stride fast enough to win some sort of endurance race. Sarah's complexion was as fair as the curly blonde hair that surrounded it and she noticed that her arms were reddening.

Lifting the case to carry it with both hands over a particularly rough patch of ground, she felt perspiration trickle between her shoulder blades. She thought back to the last time she'd been this hot. It had been in the south of France, on that same memorable holiday with her cousin Angelina, as they visited the Belliveau family. What a time they'd had. She'd brought too many foolish clothes on that excursion too. Sarah chuckled, remembering the memory happily, until she thought of Raphaël.

Despite all efforts to eradicate him from her brain, Raphaël's smiling face occasionally floated through her dreams at night. One couldn't control their dreams, after all.

As a culmination of the visit to Provence, Angelina

had married the handsome Julien Belliveau, Raphaël's brother. Sarah hadn't seen her cousin for a long time. She'd even missed their wedding since university was just ramping up in Canada at that time. It was something she regretted bitterly.

Sarah came back to the present with a jolt as she stopped on the Azure Trail to catch her breath. Pushing a strand of waist-length, curly hair from where it had become stuck on her cheek, she used the hem of her blouse to mop her face. Not very lady-like, she realised, tucking it back into her waistband, but the end justified the means.

Despite her best efforts, Gemma was long gone. So, Sarah took a few moments longer to breathe. Moving to the side of the trail, she leaned heavily on a tree and panted. She'd lugged her bag up flight after flight of uneven steps chiselled into the stone and dragged it over rocks, roots, and rubble. Surely it couldn't be much farther. She lurched onward, hopeful.

Soon she came to a small wooden hut where a man sat fanning himself with a leaflet. He asked for her ticket to pass into the National Park. Producing it, she told him haltingly between puffs that she was lodging at a place called, The Point, just ahead. He waved her through.

Gazing at the grape vines that clung to the hillside above and below her, she passed through a small valley. Sarah knew the beautiful views she should be enjoying were hindered by her exhaustion and she felt sorry for it. The scenery was really gorgeous, but heat, thirst, and fatigue were all that consumed her now. She wished fervently for a drink of water. Hefting the suitcase, she now hated with a burning passion into her arms, she stumbled around a bend.

"Just keep putting one foot in front of the other," she said aloud. "You can do this." Then, suddenly she was overlooking the open sea. She stopped again, gaping in astonishment. The cliff fell away at her feet leaving her to feel as though she were dangling at the edge of the most beautiful precipice she had ever seen.

The sapphire waters of the Ligurian Sea sparkled in the sunlight, stretching to the horizon as far as she could see. A few clouds puffed across the sky, mirroring the deep blue waves that licked the rocky shores far below. Waves crashed over them in a white frothy spray. She heard the plaintive cry of seagulls and the endless chatter of cicadas in the trees behind her. Taking it all in, she pulled the fresh sea breeze into her lungs.

Her eyes glazed with tears. In the distance to her right, the scattered, colourful houses of Vernazza poked from the rock and native trees, extending to perch precariously along the promontory of solid, jagged stone that angled to the sea.

"Oh, it's too pretty to be true," she breathed. "I am *so* grateful to be here." Sarah lingered a moment longer and then, reluctantly she lifted the suitcase into her arms again and marched on. With a lifting of her heart, she saw a tiny white sign, tacked to the side of a rock, and knew she'd arrived.

"The Point," she murmured thankfully. Lifting the latch of a small wooden gate in need of paint, she left the path and looked up a narrow path where a large stone house hunkered above her in the pines and other assorted trees. The walkway was smoother now. Spiny cactus sprang from the rocky soil while potted plants filled with bright pink flowers and red geraniums lined her way. Overlooking the Ligurian Sea, to the west of the house there was a broad, raised patio with umbrellas shading several tables. Above it was a smaller terrace that Sarah assumed must serve the guest bedrooms.

Finally, she came to the platform leading to the entrance. It consisted of two, medieval-looking, wooden doors painted a bright glossy red and held in place by large metal fixtures. Lights hung from the stone wall on either side. Overtop, wisteria clung to the width of the dwelling, reaching to encircle the red-shuttered windows gracing the top level. As she stumbled up the flight of steps, decorated with an assortment of other bright flowers, Sarah wondered if one of those windows would be her room.

She set her suitcase down with a thump, extended the handle, and bumped it over the wooden slats to the slightly ajar door. Inside she could hear Gemma's voice. Hooray! She'd done it. Placing a hand against the heavy wood, she knocked, pulled it wide, and stepped tentatively into a large kitchen.

"*Benvenuto a casa nostra*," a booming male voice called. As Sarah's eyes adjusted to the lack of light, a man leaped to attention, her shoulders were grasped, and she was drawn forward to receive three kisses that landed somewhere in the air next to her cheeks. She made out the hazy figures of the man and two others.

"*Ciao*," she replied with a smile. Standing her suitcase on its end, she included the man's wife in her greeting as the lady stepped forward with a similar welcome including a light kiss next to each of Sarah's cheeks. The couple looked young, perhaps in their early thirties. Somehow, she had expected older people to be running a bed and breakfast. The man was medium height with a shaved head and warm brown eyes in a tanned face that crinkled with smiles. He wore sandals, a floppy, short-sleeved blue button-up and a pair of brown shorts coming so far past his knees he looked like he was wearing regular pants that had shrunk, badly.

His wife was significantly shorter. She was plump and wore a sundress of bright purple that set off her dark hair and eyes. Her full red lips parted in an equally friendly grin.

"I am Romeo," the man said with a slight French accent, "and this is my wife, Luna. It is fitting do you not think so? Romeo and the moon..." He lifted his hand toward the ceiling as though the moon were visible at this very moment, then paused to wait for Sarah's response. She nodded in smiling agreement, having the impression he must ask every guest this very same question.

"It is so nice to meet you," she said. "I'm Sarah Peterson." She dragged a hand across her flushed face and took a breath before continuing. "I'm happy to be here."

"Please, come in and sit down," Luna said, resting a consoling hand on her arm. "You must be worn out."

Gemma joined them with a broad grin and Sarah couldn't help but feel a twinge of irritation with the girl. They'd lived in the same boarding house in La Spezia. Surely her friend should have told her to bring a backpack when she'd known full well they were staying halfway up a mountain.

Romeo lifted her suitcase in surprise. "You carried this up here? I am so sorry, *signorina*. That must have been terrible for you." He turned to consult with a fifth occupant of the room that Sarah hadn't noticed. A tall man stood in a wide arched entry at the far end of the kitchen, shrouded in shadow.

"Look what this girl carried!" Romeo hefted the case higher to show the man who appeared to move into the room with slow, deliberate steps.

Gemma jammed her elbow into Sarah's heaving ribcage and hissed in an undertone, "That guy is hot. Wonder if he's married?"

Sarah couldn't care less whether the guy was hot or not. She was sticky, puffing, and annoyed. But she plastered another smile on her reddened, panting face and held out an indifferent hand as the man walked toward her.

"So pleasant to see you again, Sarah," said a deep voice in a stiff French accent, taking her hand with only his fingertips.

Sarah knew that voice. It hit her like a thunderbolt from her past. Her head flew back and her mouth opened in a shriek.

"Raphaël!"

She felt her knees give out from under her and heard the sound of a chair scraping across the floor as someone rushed to grab her arm and help her sit down. She dropped onto it.

"W-what—what are you doing here?" She stared at him, her heart racing. Lifting a hand to push the hair from her eyes, she tried to focus. It was him, but she couldn't quite believe it. The room began to spin.

"Get this girl something to drink," Romeo barked.

But everything went dark as Raphaël's voice, as though reaching out from her dream world, said coldly. "I'd like to ask you the same thing."

CHAPTER 3

A glass was pressed to Sarah's mouth and the cool sensation of water touched her parched lips. Her eyes fluttered open. She pushed the glass away and came upright on the chair, her back stiffening. With a giddy sense of fantasy, she scanned the room, looking for him. Raphaël had been here—hadn't he? Where was he now? Or had she been dreaming? Her eyes came to rest on Gemma's worried face.

"Are you alright?" She held the glass out to Sarah again. "Here, take a drink. I've never seen a person pass out before."

Sarah reached for the drink and drained it. The couple, Romeo and Luna, were nearby, their faces anxious with concern.

"Can you walk?" the lady asked her. "Perhaps I could show you to your room and you could rest for a while." She nodded in encouragement. Turning to her husband she said something in Italian. The man grasped Sarah's case and disappeared through the doorway where

Raphaël had just stood. Sarah shook her head to clear the fog.

Frowning, she tried to make sense of what had just happened. Struggling to speak, she opened her mouth to ask her host the question she most wanted to know, but the words would not come. She cleared her throat and collected herself to try again. "Was—was that Raphaël Belliveau?"

"*Sì, naturalmente*," the lady frowned as she replied. "How do you know 'im? This is most strange."

"His brother is married to my cousin." Sarah said, barely above a whisper.

Luna patted her shoulder and said, "You are right. What an amazing coincidence, but don't worry about it now." She shrugged and continued. "We know Raphaël well. He and Romeo attended school together. Romeo's family are from France, but I suppose you must know that." She gave Sarah a puzzled look. "The men have been friends since they were only boys. Raphaël visits us once or twice a year, without fail." Luna held out both hands to Sarah and planted herself sturdily in front of her. "Now, let's get you to your bedroom and you can settle in. The view from your window is *fantastica*," she concluded, rolling her eyes heavenward.

Gemma retrieved the glass and Sarah allowed herself to be hauled to her feet. It was a lot to take in. Raphaël was here and staying at the same B&B. What were the odds of that happening? It was too fantastic to contemplate. She managed a wobbly smile.

"I'm fine now. It was just the walk up the hill with my luggage, the heat, and the shock of seeing..." Her voice trailed off.

"Well, he seemed just as shocked to see you," Luna said in a mothering voice as she tucked her arm beneath Sarah's and led her to the arched red-brick doorway across the kitchen. "He 'ad to leave. To meet someone in the village, you see, so you won't run into him again for a while." Luna withdrew her arm and reached to the wall where several sets of keys hung on a rack. She selected two and gestured for the girls to follow her.

Gemma scooped up her backpack and joined them.

"Sorry I left you behind on the trail," she hissed as she fell into step with Sarah. "You look awful."

"That's real nice of you," Sarah whispered sarcastically. "It's hard to look your best when you've just scaled a mountain in the blazing heat lugging thirty pounds of dead weight."

Gemma giggled. "Please forgive me." She slid an arm around Sarah's shoulders. "Lie down for a while and then we'll go exploring if you want. I promise, I'll make it up to you. Dinner's on me tonight. They don't serve anything but breakfast here, so we'll have to walk down to the village to eat."

"Okay." Sarah whispered back as they entered the dining room.

Gemma leaned close to her ear and muttered. "And what's the scoop on the hot guy? I need answers...but I'll be patient and let you tell me about him once you've had a rest."

"Thanks ever so much." Sarah's response was as sarcastic as before, but Gemma didn't appear to notice. She pulled into the lead behind Luna.

The kitchen had been a blur to Sarah, apart from red floor tiles. As she passed through the dining hall she saw a long, rustic table adorned by a huge vase of pink and deep orange dahlias with long-stemmed white lilies. They filled the room with a scent that Sarah breathed in like manna from Heaven. Pulled up to the table were padded benches, while extra chairs were set against the wall.

Over the dining table hung an ornate chandelier of wrought iron affixed to gleaming, roughly hewn wooden beams that ran from one end of the room to the other. Further above those were beams running in the opposite direction. The walls were white and mostly bare. Two enormous, decorative urns, filled with dried flowers and grasses, flanked a sideboard. She assumed it must be used to offer food to their guests at breakfast.

The same brick-coloured, ceramic-tiled floor lent a warmth to the otherwise stark and rather oppressive room, and a mottled red carpet ran narrowly down the center, underneath the table. However, the focal point of the space was along the west wall where two sets of latticed glass doors framed the beauty beyond and opened onto the patio.

As they passed through the room, Luna nodded at the table, "This is where you will come for *la colazione*," she flashed a smile over her shoulder and explained. "That is how you say breakfast, in English. It is served between the hours of seven and nine each morning. Would you like me to make coffee for you at that time?"

"Yes, please," both young women answered.

Sarah still felt faint, but with movement she revived. A good thing too, since as they ducked through a smaller archway at the end of the room, a set of whitewashed steps curved away from them up to the next floor.

However without her suitcase, it was an easy climb and Sarah reached the top beside Gemma. Luna turned to place a set of keys into her hand, and waved at two doors, one yellow and the other blue. Sarah's silver suitcase sat waiting for her outside the door painted a cheerful lemon-yellow.

"Yes," she said, nodding at Sarah. "That one is yours and the blue room is for Gemma. The large key works in this lock and the smaller one is for the downstairs entrance. We lock up at 10 each night, but you are welcome to return later than that. Please just make sure that everything is bolted behind you." The woman bobbed her head.

"*Grazie*," Sarah managed. "You have a lovely home." The lady beamed at her before handing the second set of keys to Gemma and addressing them both again.

"There are four rooms in total as you can see on the opposite side." She gestured to the opposite side of the hallway where there was a mint green door and a rose-coloured one. Luna took a breath and began what was clearly a short, rehearsed speech. "Romeo and I have compiled a folder of information for each room. You will find it beside the bed. It contains the rules of the house and suggestions for favourite restaurants, *gelaterias*, walks, and other sights you might wish to take in while you are here. I hope you enjoy your stay." Luna smoothed hands over her ample waist and bustled downstairs.

The girls grinned at one another. All irritation fled

from Sarah as Gemma stepped forward and enveloped her in a hug.

"I'm really sorry about the trouble you had getting here, but things will only get better now. And I'll help you get that horrible case down to the train when we leave." She held Sarah at arm's length and looked into her eyes. "Okay?"

"Okay." Sarah moved toward her door and jangled the keys. "I can't wait to see what my room is like."

Gemma laughed and fitted a key into her own lock. "Me too. Is an hour enough time to rest and get settled?" She glanced back.

"Plenty." Sarah slid the key in and turned the handle. Grabbing the offensive luggage, she dragged it into the room behind her.

More of the enormous wood beams greeted her inside, but this time they were at a decided slant. The lowest point ended just over a set of double glass doors to her left. She was directly beneath the roof of the house. A single bed, draped with delicate white material and dotted with sprigs of tiny yellow flowers, sat at the center of the room. An antique bureau stood sturdily on the high side, to the right. Straight ahead, and to the right of the bed, were two latticed windows each swathed with the same fabric as the bed. However, the long windows to her left were what garnered her attention. They were actually glass doors leading to the upper terrace she'd noticed from outside. Throw rugs ornamented the floor on either side and at the end of the bed, while two end tables each supported a lamp.

"Tyler would hate this place," she breathed. "But I love it."

Dropping her things to the floor, she rushed to the terrace door, drew the curtains away, and opened it to peer outside. Granted, she noticed the terrace was shared with another room just down from hers, but it was glorious nonetheless. A thin iron railing ran around the perimeter of the outdoor space. Lanky pine trees obscured part of the view, but she could still see where the Ligurian Sea sparkled in the distance. It was blue as far as she could see. Leaning her elbows on the railing, she closed her eyes and listened to the distant echo of voices working in the vineyards and the soothing swish of water lapping on rocks far below.

With joy bubbling up in her heart, she strode back inside, kicked off her shoes, and stretched her toes luxuriously before tearing the elastic from her hair to run fingers through the tangled strands. She turned to the task at hand, emptying the hateful suitcase and hanging her clothes in a tall wardrobe beside the yellow door. Then, just maybe, there would be time to test that inviting-looking bed.

"Sarah! Are you awake?"

The voice interrupted her dream, and she rolled over, blocking out the sound with a pillow and striving to hold onto her vision just a moment longer.

She stood on a wind-swept beach, her hair and dress streaming behind her as she stared longingly out to sea. The world was asleep. Overhead, a garland of stars glittered from a canopy of midnight blue as the moon drifted from the cover of a cloud. It gleamed upon the gently lapping waves, turning whitecaps a luminescent silver. Behind her, the twinkling lights of Vernazza lay in purple shadow.

A boat came into view. It was small, like the sort that fishermen used. But standing at the prow was a man she knew, the man she waited for. He was dark-haired and handsome. His white shirt, open at the throat, reflected the moon's glow and his sleeves were rolled over muscular arms she knew would be darkened from labour beneath a relentless sun. His teeth flashed white. She loved that smile. His liquid brown eyes found her, despite the deepening shades of evening that hid her slender form along the rocky shore.

"My dear, do you watch for me?" he asked, in his familiar husky voice. Extending his hand, he beckoned her to join him as his craft bobbed ever closer. She lifted her arms at once, running to him, her heart flooding with happiness. She'd known he would come for her, and now he had arrived. She opened her mouth to answer...

"Sarah!" Gemma's voice was insistent. She hammered a fist on the door. "You've been sleeping for two hours. We have to go now or a whole day will be wasted."

Sarah jerked upright with a groan. Flinging her legs over the edge of the bed, she answered, "Sorry. I'm up now. Give me two minutes."

Gemma thumped downstairs as Sarah flew to the adjoining bathroom to splash water on her face. Yanking a lemon-coloured towel from a rack, she patted dry and examined herself in the mirror. A youthful face peered back at her—slightly freckled creamy complexion, blue eyes, and curly blonde hair cascaded down her back. But there was a faded look to her eyes and purple shadows where there hadn't been any before. Sarah frowned. She would rest while she was here and be good as new when she went home. Even though she hadn't strayed far from the city of La Spezia where she'd been working, she would make up for it now.

Thoughts of Tyler surfaced as she tugged a wide-toothed comb through her locks and rummaged through the drawer where she'd put a pair of jean shorts and a mauve t-shirt. Pulling them on, she laid the skirt and blouse on her bed to be washed later, and considered the man who had asked her to be his wife.

He was funny, if a little intense, loving, and kind. Although he wasn't much for hiking, she knew he loved seafood and good wine, which was in abundance here and would probably enjoy the Cinque Terre—with someone else.

Sarah bent over her suitcase to remove the heavy-duty sandals she'd brought and should have strapped on this morning before they left. Flopping onto her bed to slide them on her feet, she paused. Of course, in thinking about him she realised she was trying not to think of the dream.

The man in her dream, the one who evoked such passion and longing in her heart, wasn't Tyler. It was someone who'd entered her dream world before, so many times.

It was Raphaël Belliveau.

CHAPTER 4

It didn't take long for the two girls to hurry down the path toward Vernazza. Sarah kept her mind occupied with the view, which wasn't hard, and with watching where she walked lest she tumble down the steep incline. She wouldn't allow herself to think about the dream or the dark-haired man who had starred in it, feeling sure it had been brought on by the shock of seeing Raphaël again, nothing more. She would devote herself to enjoying this last week with her friend.

"So, I want details on who that guy was and why you fainted over him?" Gemma demanded as soon as they were able to walk side-by-side. Sarah looked at her, pleased to note that Gemma had left the ball cap behind and had brushed her chestnut hair until it shone in the late day sun. She'd also changed out of her boots and now wore sensible sandals with a sleeveless, lemon-yellow romper which was just about the most feminine clothing Sarah had ever seen her wear.

Sarah sighed. She'd been dreading this. "His name is

Raphaël Belliveau. You heard me explain to Luna that his brother, Julien, married my cousin, right? I told you the whole story, years ago. About how Angelina and I went to visit Julien and his mother in Provence...and the two of them fell in love."

Gemma slowed her gait as she digested the information. "Oh." Recognition dawned on her face. "He's the brother you fell madly in love with." She reached out to grab Sarah's arm and pulled her to a stop. "The man you've never quite gotten over. Am I right?" Gemma was nearly dancing with excitement.

"Yes. Ugh...No. Sort of," Sarah dragged a tired hand across her brow, unconsciously rubbing at the furrows between her eyes. "I was a foolish girl. We fell in love, yes. He wanted me to stay in France and live at the chateau for a few months, so we could get to know one another better." She paused and stared past Gemma at the sparkling sea. "But I was stupid. I was too absorbed with dating every guy that paid me a compliment or looked at me sideways. So, I returned to Canada, ended the relationship abruptly, hurt Raphaël, and started dating someone who wasn't half the man he was." It pained her to retell the story again, especially as she still remembered crying over it when she'd told Gemma the whole unhappy tale years before.

"Can we go now?" she asked. Sidestepping around her friend, Sarah continued walking.

"Maybe this is destiny," Gemma said, catching up and plucking at the sleeve of Sarah's top.

"What?" Sarah stopped this time and rounded on her friend with a scowl. "What are you saying? That I was meant to meet Raphaël here?"

"Yeah, kind of," Gemma's eyes were wide. "What if you two are destined to be together? Maybe the universe placed you both here to offer a second chance at true love."

"Didn't you hear me?" Sarah retorted. "I hurt him—badly. He doesn't want anything to do with me, you must have seen that earlier. Even as I passed out at his feet I could feel the dislike rolling off him in waves. Those feelings are dead. Besides, I have to deal with one man before I can even think of dating another. He's not letting go."

"Okay, I get that, but I warned you this would happen with Tyler. He has a one-track mind." Gemma tapped her forehead with a finger. "Maybe Raphaël is your second chance at happiness. You're here and Tyler's in Canada, so why worry about him. I think seeing Raphaël is predestination."

"Look," Sarah interrupted sharply, "I'm not discussing this any further. It's just some crazy fluke that we happen to be staying at the same B&B as him. I agree it defies all probability, but that doesn't mean I'm supposed to fling myself at him." She turned away and opened the small gate leading to the main trail. "I don't want anyone in my life. Now let's go."

Gemma said nothing more on the subject, but Sarah's thoughts were reeling. If she was going to get harassed about Raphaël, she would regret she'd ever agreed to this brief holiday. She squashed any niggling thoughts about Raphaël, and focused her attention on the path.

They passed a few red-faced hikers slogging up the grade beneath the weight of their backpacks. Sarah grinned. None of those people were clasping an enormous rolling suitcase to their chests, as she had done. They looked tired, but everyone smiled jauntily. It would be hard to be unhappy in the Cinque Terre.

The sun was gliding through the eastern sky. Soon, it would slip behind the mountain. Trains would carry flocks of tourists back to the predictable, air-conditioned hotels of the city, leaving the hustle and bustle in the tiny village of Vernazza to die away.

Sarah knew it would happen. Only one other time, during this entire summer, had she ventured outside of La Spezia. She'd gone to see the Leaning Tower of Pisa with Gemma. During the day, tour buses and trains discharged their cargo by the hundreds at the famous destination. She'd read that over five million people visited Pisa each year which turned the area, particularly around the tower, into a congested sea of humanity. To manage the crowds, she and her friend had stayed overnight.

When buses and trains pulled out in the evening, carrying away the majority of tourists, the city took on a different feel. It relaxed. As though Pisa itself had taken a deep, cleansing breath, the streets stilled, and Italians came out to enjoy their city once the day's work was done. She and Gemma had soaked up the local atmosphere, enjoyed a drink at an *aperitivo* bar, and had eaten in a fabulous restaurant before strolling around the famous sights under a starry sky.

She gazed down at Vernazza, expecting the same phenomenon to take place here. Jolted from her reverie by one of the knobby tree roots that crossed the well-trodden path, she recovered her balance and realised she was still feeling tired. Teaching English for the summer had been a wonderful experience, but she had thrown all of her energy into it, taking little time for herself. This last week, she decided, would be devoted to seeing something of Italy rather than the inside of a classroom.

As they neared the village, Sarah and Gemma passed houses built into the side of the rock, leaving only their red roof tiles to be seen at ground level. Rows of terraced grape vines stretched everywhere and olive trees were abundant. Sarah had missed all this on her way up. The scratchy sound of the cicadas was omnipresent as well, but the noise blended so perfectly into the surroundings that it was nothing more than a soothing accompaniment to the beautiful Italian scenery.

There wasn't any breeze and the sun beat relentlessly against the back of her neck and arms, but this time Sarah wasn't worried. She'd borrowed sunscreen from Gemma and would buy some for herself once she found a *farmacia* in the village. Knowing the Italian form of the word pharmacy made her happy. She hummed a little tune as they veered off the main path and began to wind along a narrow, cobblestone lane toward the pastel-coloured houses that rose in a jumbled fashion to form the town. Maybe she could just avoid Raphaël completely and enjoy herself.

Running beside them on their left was a high, ancient-looking stone wall. Straight ahead Sarah could see the sea and the continuation of the Italian Riviera. However, it was dangerous to gape at her environment too much as the path beneath her feet was so uneven.

At any given time, it would turn to steps, roughly hewn from the rock, and then back again to an uneven trail.

The path dropped in among the houses now and they threaded their way along a constricted walkway. Finally, they stepped onto Via Roma, the main street of town. Sarah gazed about with pleasure.

The area was bustling with life. Tiny shops lined the street, their wares spilling into the pedestrian path. There were eye-catching racks of gleaming leather shoes, light-coloured clothing to ward off the heat, hand-made jewelry, and brightly arranged flowers. Sarah took a deep breath. It was a festival for the senses.

The air was infused with a pleasing mixture of garlic and seafood, focaccia bread baking, and the tang of sea air. She clasped her hands with joy, then hurried to catch up to Gemma who had taken it all in stride and was following the majority of people on their way to find the waterfront. At least it appeared that was where they were going. It wouldn't be a good idea to lose her friend since Sarah knew her sense of direction often failed her. She didn't want to waste time wandering down alleys in search of Gemma.

As the street became more constricted, she walked behind, but as she was taller, she peered over her chum's head. The narrow lane between buildings suddenly opened to an expanse of pavement where multi-coloured umbrellas were placed along the beachfront, enticing thirsty travellers to sit down, enjoy the view, and have a glass of wine. In front of that was a small, V-shaped expanse of sand where families splashed in the waves. A long, rocky promontory to their left curved into the sea where a line of small boats was tethered.

On their right, a jumble of tall, colourful houses rose into the evening air. She craned her neck to see what looked like a bell tower reflecting the setting sun.

People lounged on deck chairs, snapped photos, and enjoyed life. Sarah stood beside Gemma, quietly taking it all in.

"Awesome, isn't it?" Gemma said, for once her tone sounding awed. "Glad we came?"

"I'll always be glad." Sarah whispered. She lifted a hand to shade her eyes as she stared at iridescent waves gently lapping the sandy shore. "Thanks for encouraging me to listen to my heart, rather than my sense of duty."

"You're welcome." Gemma twirled around to grin, her short brown hair bouncing. "You wanted to look for a pharmacy, right? I saw one on the street we just walked down."

It only took ten minutes to buy a few essentials, most importantly sunscreen for Sarah, and then they were off again.

"Now, I'm hungry and..." Gemma consulted her phone, "it's almost seven. At least a few restaurants should be opening soon. Shall we find one?"

"We shall," Sarah agreed. "But let's look for somewhere a little quieter. Maybe a place not quite so full of tourists, if that's possible."

"Agreed." Gemma plunged back into the stream of people who were making their way to the seafront, dodging and angling her way to where the street was broader. Then, she swung down the first opening to her left, with Sarah on her heels.

Down a cramped passage, bereft of the scads of people found elsewhere in the town, they spotted an unassuming restaurant with paint peeling from the pale orange walls. Several white umbrellas had been placed over top of small square tables out front. A stone barrier, hanging with lush green vines, ran around one half of the outside eating space. At the other end a lone palm tree almost appeared to spring from the cobblestones and more tables were set beneath its leafy fronds. The place looked inviting and friendly.

The clink and clatter from a busy kitchen rose into the air. The girls took these as good signs, not to mention the wonderful smells emanating from an open door. They walked toward it, tentatively waiting for someone to greet them.

A smiling older man with graying hair and a stiff white apron appeared through the low entrance and scurried toward them, grabbing two menus from a basket.

"*Banasura, buonasera*," he cried, waving an arm in welcome. "*Inglese?*" He paused to look questioningly at them.

Both Sarah and Gemma nodded. They must really look English.

The man clasped the cards to his chest and continued in a sing-song voice. "Inside or outside?"

"I think, inside," Gemma responded, with a glance to Sarah for approval.

Taking off their sun hats and removing sunglasses, as it was dark inside the restaurant, they followed the waiter's quick steps to a small table in the corner. It was charming. The entire building was made of stone. Mirrors hung on each wall, reflecting the few yellowish tulip-shaped light covers that added to the soft ambiance. Tables were small, painted white, covered with linen cloths, and pushed closely together. Sarah had found space was at a premium in Europe, but she was used to the close proximity and enjoyed it.

"*Grazie*," they said in unison as he pulled out their chairs and handed them menus with a flourish. He then stood back with an indulgent smile.

"*Signorinas...Vuoi da bere?*" His eyebrows lifted enquiringly as he looked from one to the other. It was obvious the man wasn't fluent in English. Both Gemma and Sarah spoke slowly to make the language barrier as easy on him as they could.

"*Acqua per favore*," said Gemma, wiping her brow in an exaggerated show for the benefit of their waiter. "I am so *assetata*...thirsty." He nodded and turned to Sarah.

"*Vino della casa, per favore*," said Sarah. The man marched away to fulfill their orders. Giggling, Sarah said in an undertone, "There are certain phrases it's been necessary to learn in Italian, wouldn't you agree? Requests for water and wine top the list." Gemma smiled her agreement as she bent to read the menu.

Sarah also perused the card the man had given her, realizing with a sinking heart that it was all in Italian. Her abilities only went so far. It was more authentic to get off the beaten path and join the locals for dinner, but those sorts of menu were seldom translated into English. Oh well, time to consult Google.

Teaching English to adults in La Spezia had meant there was an opportunity to learn some Italian. As a result, she had picked up quite a few words, but not enough to read an intricate list of dinner items. Gemma was only slightly better.

"Warm octopus and potato salad." Sarah read a translation aloud.

"Sounds good to me," Gemma declared. "I'll try anything once."

Sarah rolled her eyes with a chuckle. "Is that why you dated Jacob?"

Gemma snickered before sobering. "Yeah, that was a mistake."

Jacob had been the young man Gemma was seeing when she'd met Sarah at university. Gemma had been quite serious about creating a future with him until she'd found he was going out with two other girls at the same time. She'd ended the relationship immediately and avoided men since then.

"At least *you* made a match for yourself with Tyler." She batted her eyes at Sarah over the menu. "Oh, that's right, you turned him down. Maybe that was preordained too."

Sarah studied the menu, the subject making her uncomfortable. She tapped another food item into her phone and smiled at her friend. "This sounds good. I didn't even need to translate...Pasta Al Pesto."

"I dunno," Gemma looked comically doubtful. "It'll have to be pretty great to beat a warm octopus."

"On potatoes," finished Sarah. The two girls laughed. Sarah was relieved her friend's focus had been diverted. Both looked up as the waiter arrived with their drinks on a tray. Easing a tall stemmed glass of red wine onto the spotless tablecloth in front of her, and setting a glass and small pitcher of water down for Gemma. He slid the tray under his arm and struck a match he pulled from his pocket. Lighting a candle on the table between them, he stepped back to await their order.

With a mixture of halting Italian and pointing, the girls conveyed their requests and thanked him. With a slight bow the server collected the menus and hurried away.

Sarah leaned her elbows on the table and rested her chin in her hands to watch a steady stream of customers line up outside the restaurant. She felt pleased. Only places that offered good food were popular. It appeared they had chosen well.

With a shock wave that rippled through her body like electricity, she recognized someone in the waiting crowd outside.

Not Raphaël, again! But it *was* him. He had a beautiful woman at his side, her bare arm linked through his as they crossed the threshold and were led to a table for two near the door.

Involuntarily, Sarah slid down in her seat. Thankfully they were sitting in a shadowed corner, but still, she was facing them. She scraped her chair across the tiled floor so as to be partially obscured behind Gemma. From that vantage point, she unabashedly stared at Raphaël and the mystery lady.

"What is it?" Gemma whispered, swivelling in her seat to see what had captured Sarah's attention.

"Don't look!" Sarah hissed, sinking even lower in her seat. "It's Raphaël and some gorgeous woman in a red dress. They just came in."

"What!" Gemma stiffened. "Is there nowhere safe for you?" She looked at Sarah thoughtfully. "Hmm..."

"No! Don't start," Sarah hissed, wishing she had the

menu to hold in front of her face. "It's a tiny village okay. We're bound to run into him. Besides, he has Wonder Woman with him. The man's not here to pick up on some past romance with me."

Sarah lifted her wine and took a gulp as she continued her rant. "I can't believe he's staying in Vernazza though," she muttered. "How could that happen? I mean, I knew he had friends in Italy, but out of the whole country they had to be here! It's ridiculous. Even if he was in the Cinque Terre it would have been a wild coincidence, but in Vernazza and at the same B&B? What are the chances we would have rented rooms from *his* friends?" she demanded of her friend. "And at the very same time he was visiting? It's preposterous."

"Relax. He's not exactly jumping you, now is he?" Gemma leaned back in her chair, took her napkin, and laid it carefully across her lap. "Who cares about him? We came here to enjoy ourselves and that's what we're going to do." Gemma held up her water for a toast. "Deal?"

"Deal," Sarah said without conviction. Still slumped in her seat, she clinked glasses and took another deep swig of her wine.

"Hey! You better slow down." Gemma looked at her in mock horror. "I can't carry you back up the hill, you know."

Sarah tore her gaze away from Raphaël and focused on her companion. "You're right. I won't let it bother me. I'm putting it out of my mind," she said carelessly. "So, what shall we do tomorrow?"

But as Gemma outlined the ideas she had for their first real day in the Cinque Terre, Sarah's eyes were drawn back to the couple seated by the window. Raphaël looked, if anything, handsomer than she'd remembered. His hair was longer, swept away from his face in dark swaths, and his tanned face was animated as he described something to his date with hand gestures that made her laugh delightedly. He wore a crisp, white button-up shirt over snug fitting jeans belted at his trim waist. The sleeves were rolled up to his elbows revealing tanned, muscular forearms.

Sarah's heart skipped a beat when his eyes flicked her way. She shuffled sideways in her chair. Had he seen her? She didn't think so. Cautiously she edged back to look at him again, feeling disoriented. It was as if the last five years had melted away and here was Raphaël again, young, vital, and as handsome as ever. A sudden ache in the region of her heart surprised her. If not for her foolish choices, that might have been her sitting with Raphaël. How different life would have been. She watched him for a few moments longer, feeling their history and a strange longing for something that was no longer possible.

The woman he shared the table with was beautiful, Sarah thought unhappily, staring at her over the flickering flame of the candle. The least Raphaël could do would be to date an ugly woman. Unfortunately, though the dress this woman wore skimmed a voluptuous figure. Every part of her was shapely starting with her matching stilettoes all the way up to her full, fire-engine red lips. Her hair was dark as ebony and curled softly past the middle of her back, and she fluttered long lashes in a heart-shaped face as she reached across the table for Raphaël's hand.

Sarah had a horrible thought. *What if the woman was his wife!* With a stab of pain, she leaned back and her body sagged.

"What's wrong now?" Gemma asked. "Have you listened to a word I've said?"

Pulling herself together, Sarah took a deep, calming breath and concentrated on her chum. Raphaël could live and do as he pleased. The man was nothing to her. She hoped he was very happy.

"Sorry," she said. "I was distracted, but it won't happen again. You have my full attention."

Sarah refused to allow herself even one more glance toward the table by the door as she chatted with Gemma about all there was to see and do over the next four days. When their food arrived, they both giggled at the sight of the grilled tentacles curled over a bed of mashed potatoes with a garnish of broccoli. This was one time in her life where Sarah did *not* wish she'd ordered the same thing.

Later, she dabbed her mouth with a napkin and drained the last of her second glass of wine. Stealing a glance toward Raphaël, she was relieved to see the couple had left. She set the glass down, opened her bag to reach her phone, and checked the time.

Grinning at Gemma, she said. "Shall we go for a late night wander through the village before we head back to our rooms?"

"Naturally." Gemma pushed back her chair and stood with a stretch. They'd settled the bill earlier and now strolled out the door beneath a darkened sky. She looked up and pointed. "There's going to be a full moon in a few nights. Strange things can happen under a full moon, you know."

Sarah quickened her step. She knew what Gemma was getting at and decided to change the conversation. "Did you ever notice how kids seem to sense the full moon?"

"That's true." Gemma laughed. "I had a whole class howling at it last spring during my internship."

Slowly, they retraced their steps back to the harbour, sharing funny situations that had arisen while finishing their degrees working as student teachers in elementary schools. In no time at all they were standing in the harbour, staring out to sea. Since they'd taken so long, the sun had disappeared. Although there were a few streetlights, it was getting dim, and they turned away from the beach area to make their way back to the B&B before it became too dark. Next time, Sarah thought, they would need to buy a flashlight in case they were out late.

As Sarah followed Gemma around the corner of a building near the beach, two shapes loomed up before them and her friend walked full tilt into people out for a similar evening stroll. Gemma staggered backward and her purse, loosely looped over her arm, dropped to the pavement.

"*Oh la-la!*" said a high-pitched female voice. "*Je suis désolé*.

"It's no problem," Gemma replied, snatching up her bag and stepping into the light. "Oh, it's you," she said in shocked tones as she looked into the faces of her would-be assailants.

Sarah stopped herself from turning tail and

marching in the opposite direction. The overhead lamp had revealed Raphaël and his gorgeous companion.

"Raphaël! It is the two girls you were telling me about," the woman said with infuriating good humour. "Won't you introduce us?'

With an audible sigh, Raphaël stepped forward. "Gabrielle, I would like you to meet Sarah Peterson and 'er friend..." he left an opening for Sarah to pick up the introduction.

"...And my friend, Gemma Mark," Sarah said. "I'm pleased to meet you, Gabrielle." Stepping forward she thrust out her hand. Instead, the young woman grasped Sarah's shoulders and kissed her cheeks three times in rapid succession. *La bise*, Sarah knew, was the typical French greeting and one which she had almost forgotten about. It was charmingly unexpected, and she smiled despite herself.

"But Raphaël tells me you are 'is friend and 'is friend is mine friend also," Gabrielle said in a lilting voice before greeting Gemma in the same manner. "I am 'appy to meet you both. We saw you in the restaurant, but Raphaël said we should not disturb your meal. Silly boy," she giggled and gave his arm a playful slap. Sarah could see her teeth flash white in the golden ring of light beneath the lamp.

"You only arrived in Vernazza today?" Gabrielle asked. The woman appeared genuinely pleased to make their acquaintance.

"Yes. How about you?" Gemma began making friends immediately, as was her way. Sarah rolled her eyes in the darkness. She'd watched Gemma do it at university a hundred times. Only before it had been great and had gotten the girls invited to parties, free meals, concerts, and even wedding receptions. This time it was different. Sarah wanted no part of a friendship involving Raphaël and his girlfriend or wife. Gemma knew that too. What was she thinking?

"We're going to walk to Monterosso al Mare tomorrow. Do you know anything about it? Where should we eat?" Gemma prattled on in her usual gregarious manner. Sarah fumed in the shadows.

"Raphaël, they must come with us. Invite them, *s'il te plaît*?" Gabrielle clapped her hands together in delight.

"Of course, my dear," he replied, although Sarah could hear the reluctance in his deep voice with the lovely French accent. "You are both welcome to join us in the morning. We plan to 'ike along the Azure Trail and return on the train."

"Thanks," Gemma gushed. "We'd love that, wouldn't we?" Everyone turned to stare at Sarah. She mustered a smile, forcing it onto her face with extreme effort.

In truth, she wanted to scream, NO! I don't want to go anywhere with Raphaël, and especially not with him and his gorgeous wife or girlfriend...or whatever the heck she was. This was horrible.

Instead, she answered with an even, neutral tone that even shocked her, "Yes, that would be lovely. Thank you."

As they parted and Sarah trailed after Gemma, who continued babbling about how much fun they'd have the next day, Sarah allowed her thoughts to stray.

What had just happened? Her plan was to avoid the man at all costs, not join him for a day's excursion. Was Gemma mad? Didn't her friend know what she was doing? Or was she still labouring under the delusion that it was Sarah's destiny to meet Raphaël and rekindle some dead-as-dust romance they'd shared almost five years ago.

And what was with the girlfriend? If Raphaël were her partner in life, she wouldn't be so thrilled to have their private rambles invaded by a couple of women tourists. Especially when one of them had a history with him.

She yawned despite her upset. This holiday was turning out to be more stressful and tiring than the whole summer of work she'd just completed. Tramping along in Gemma's footsteps she wondered what the next day would hold in store. Painful memories? Cold looks? Uncomfortable moments?

Or, worse than all of those, the resurrection of why she'd fallen in love with Raphaël in the first place?

CHAPTER 5

Today Sarah dressed in something appropriate for hiking in the heat, a high-waisted, short, lavender skort with a deep purple tank top. Underneath she wore her bathing suit as per Gemma's directions the night before. She dug out a small backpack to carry money, a towel, her pass for the trail and the train, and water. Then, she slathered on sunscreen, and grabbed her sunglasses with a wide-brimmed hat before tossing them behind her on the bed while she sat to tie her well-made running shoes. She yawned. Despite feeling tired the night before, she hadn't been able to sleep. Her phone had buzzed repeatedly as Tyler had tried in vain to call her. Exasperated, she'd turned it off and slid it out of sight into a drawer.

By the time she entered the dining room in the B&B, Gemma, Gabrielle, and Raphaël had finished eating. Raphaël sat next to Gabrielle, holding a small coffee cup between his hands like a prayer. With his back to Sarah, Raphaël stared out the window making no move to greet her. The two women chattered like old friends across the table.

"I was just going to come up and bang on your door," Gemma announced around a mouthful of yogurt. "This is my second helping. We've been here for ages." She grinned and lifted another spoonful in salute. Gemma had on her ubiquitous green ball cap with her ponytail poked out the back, and a baggy, mottled blue t-shirt. Sports were Gemma's thing—fashion not so much.

"*Salut*, Sarah," Gabrielle chirped. She twisted around in her chair to smile with glossy pink lips. Her long dark hair was braided into one thick rope that swung down her back. She wore a fuchsia tank top and short, matching skirt. From what Sarah could see, the woman looked fabulous again.

"I 'ope you 'ad a good sleep?" the young woman asked.

Drat this girl for being so irritatingly chipper. And pretty too.

"Sorry for being a bit late. And yes, I slept like a log." Sarah lied, smiling back at her. Gemma, she ignored. How could her friend put her in this position? She'd been wholly unrepentant last night when they'd talked. She stood at Sarah's door going on and on about fate and kismet until Sarah had told her to leave her alone and get some sleep.

Keeping her eyes averted, Sarah hurried to the sideboard, grabbed a plate, and helped herself to a croissant and a crunchy biscotti sprinkled with sliced almonds. The girls took up their conversation again.

As she made her way around the long table to sit

beside Gemma, Luna poked her head through the kitchen door.

"*Buon giorno,*" she said sunnily. "Would you like some coffee?"

"*Sì, grazie,*" Sarah answered. "Cappuccino if you have it?"

Luna raised a finger. "*Un minuto.*" She disappeared.

Sarah applied herself to the croissant first, which was fresh and flakey. She kept her eyes down, intensely aware of Raphaël who sat directly across from her. In the background, she heard the hissing of steam as her coffee was prepared. She could almost taste the alluring aroma in the air.

Moments later Luna marched into the room, an apron of gigantic proportions covering another sundress of electric green with splashy pink daisies. She sat the hot beverage in front of Sarah with a thump and stood back until she had taken a sip.

"*Delizioso,*" Sarah exclaimed. "It's so good."

Rich and frothy, she was only sorry it was so small, but knew it would be no trouble for Luna to make her a second cup if there was time. For now, she snapped off a bite of the biscotti and crunched her way through. It made so much noise, that she looked up involuntarily and caught Raphaël's eyes boring into her soul.

Her face suffused with colour as their eyes held for long seconds. Then he asked her the question she'd been waiting for. He spoke barely above a whisper, clearly believing the constant, high-pitched chatter between Gemma and Gabrielle provided enough noise to veil his query.

"Why are you here? Did you somehow know Luna

and Romeo were my friends, and that I would be visiting them? And if so, why would you come?" His eyebrows knit together in a frown.

Sarah drained her coffee cup before answering. Yes, she had regrets for what she'd done and what she'd lost when she so abruptly ended their relationship. And most certainly for how she must have hurt him. But all of that was in the past and there was nothing she could do about it now. She was sorry for her foolishness, but the suggestion that she had somehow contrived this meeting annoyed her.

"How could I possibly know where you are at any given time? I don't keep track of your movements and believe me when I say I don't keep tabs on who your friends are, Italian or otherwise," she hissed back. "All arrangements for this trip were made by Gemma. I certainly wouldn't have come here if I'd known." She banged her cup down with a little more force than she'd meant to and the other occupants of the table looked at her in surprise.

"Ready to go?" she asked brightly, shoving back her chair. Groaning under her breath, she hoped they hadn't overheard her tirade.

"*Bien sûr*. Of course." Gabrielle leapt to her feet and gathered her dishes to carry to the kitchen.

So, Gabrielle was polite as well as sweet, pretty, and friendly. It only annoyed Sarah more, taking notice of the woman's actions. This just got worse by the second. She watched as Gabrielle picked up Raphaël's dishes too, then scooted away. Sarah wasn't thrilled about it, yet she couldn't help but like the girl, whom she guessed to be about twenty years old. If that were true, at twenty-seven, Raphaël was a little old for her, but they did appear happy together.

Chancing a sideways look at Raphaël, she observed him stand and shove his chair under the table roughly, then scowl at it as though the thing had tried to take a chomp out of his leg. As he began carrying food into the kitchen to help Luna she wondered if perhaps she should have answered with a little more gentleness. Hopefully, she'd have an opportunity to talk to him again. She wanted to explain properly how sorry she was for the past, and how she was just as shocked as he was that they were both staying at the same B&B.

He did look good though. He was dressed casually today, but still managed to look attractive. At least Sarah thought so. In cream-coloured shorts that ended just above his knees and a loose, mint-green, short sleeved button-up shirt undone to the middle of his chest, he was probably the most handsome man she'd ever seen.

"Come on then," Gemma gave her a little push. "Let's fill our water bottles and set out before the sun gets too high."

Sarah nodded. "Right behind you."

"I'm going outside to the garden. It is not far so don't lock up," Luna called from the front step. "Oh. And the tap water is safe for drinking." She waved and the door slammed behind her.

Sarah made her way under the red-brick arch and into the kitchen, admiring it properly for the first time. It wasn't as large as she'd thought. Heavy beams and the red tiled floor continued throughout this part of the downstairs. The plaster walls were painted a warm mustard yellow while matching curtains, instead of doors, hid dishes and food from view. A high wooden shelf ran all around the room and it was from beneath this ledge that most of the lighting had been installed. Even though there were only two small windows, the hidden lights caused the room to glow.

Crossing to the sink, Gemma turned on the tap, unscrewed the top from her bottle, and stuck it under the cold gush of water. Gabrielle was already slipping her backpack over her shoulders, seated atop a bench near the door, and Raphaël was tapping his toe impatiently, waiting to fill his bottle next.

Sarah glanced at her phone, a reflex action to cover her nervousness, and noticed the time. Not even nine o'clock and her stomach was already in knots.

꽃

THE WALK TO MONTEROSSO AL MARE WAS LOVELY. The four of them spread out, single file, with Raphaël in the lead, followed by Gemma, and then Gabrielle. Sarah brought up the rear, which suited her just fine. She looked at the path stretching like a dusty ribbon ahead of her and thought of the feet that had walked here for centuries. No wonder Italians were slim. They didn't drive to the shopping mall and park as close as possible to the doors, like everyone she knew back home. Italians walked wherever they needed to go. Whether in the cities or villages or the countryside, these people were physically active.

However, this trail across the steep, rugged terrain of the Cinque Terre National Park, was especially gruelling. How people had done it on a regular basis when this was the only way they had to reach family in the next village, was amazing to her. She'd done a little reading on the area once she knew she was coming and had learned it wasn't until 1874 that the railway, linking all five villages, had been completed. Yet the name 'Cinque Terre' had been mentioned in a document back in the 15th century. And who knew how long it had existed before that?

To her left, and far below, lay the sparkling Ligurian Sea. Boats of all sizes hugged the shoreline, their frothy spray cutting a V-shaped wedge in the water behind them. Timeless craggy rocks reared jaggedly from where the azure waves licked at their feet, and the hills, covered in grape vines, were remarkable. Each row of terracing, carved into the cliff face, was held in place by rock walls that would have taken years to build and must still need constant repair.

The view was breathtaking. She fell behind a few times in order to take pictures and then hurried to catch up. On they trudged down steps cut into the very rock itself and past trees whose branches were bent over the walkway. There was a great diversity of landscape with many shrubs, trees, and plants that Sarah marvelled at. She knew olive trees when she saw them. They had been everywhere in Provence. But there were other, prickly looking bushes here she wasn't sure of at all.

Finally, they dropped down into the village of Monterosso. It was busier, larger, and more commercial than Vernazza. It boasted a long, sandy beach which Sarah had read was the longest in the Cinque Terre.

Over the tops of buildings and past a rail fence, she could see the iconic green and orange striped umbrellas were already set out in tidy rows with deck chairs situated beneath them.

Raphaël stopped and they gathered around him on the street. "I took the liberty of calling to reserve a spot on the left side of the lido, close to the rock that you see over there." He pointed. "They were quite booked up, but managed to make an exception. Follow me, *s'il vous plaît*."

He led them to an opening that ran along the other side of the metal fence beside the road and down an incline toward the beach. The man monitoring the gate appeared to know him and merely nodded as they passed through.

As Raphaël strode ahead, Gabrielle looked back at Sarah and Gemma. She pulled her sunglasses down to eye them over the top. "Whenever I come 'ere with Raphaël, we always ask for the same spot on Fegina Beach. It is quite scenic. You will see."

Sarah nodded and swung the backpack over her shoulder. Perspiration trickled down her back and her face felt flushed and hot. It would be great to take a swim. The aquamarine water beckoned to her.

Moments later, Raphaël threw his bag down on an extended beach chair under a colourful umbrella and looked back at them with a grin. It was the happiest Sarah had seen him yet and her heart did a little flip.

"These are yours to choose from." He motioned at the three other loungers nearby. "Please, enjoy. I think you will find this the nicest beach in the Cinque Terre."

She smiled in response as his eyes met hers. They

held for long moments until he broke free with a shake of his head and spoke. "I believe we could all use a swim to cool off and refresh ourselves after that hike. *N'est-ce pas?*" Without waiting for an answer, he dug a towel out of his bag and began to unbutton his shirt, looking out to sea.

Gemma tossed her things onto the lounger furthest from Raphaël and Gabrielle sat on the one next to him. Sarah slowly made her way to the remaining chair, trying not to stare as Raphaël pulled the light shirt from his broad shoulders and went to work on his shorts.

Pull yourself together! You're not some schoolgirl anymore. The man despises you for what you did and he should. She set her pack down and dropped onto the chair beside it.

Sarah sighed and looked up to see Gemma and Gabrielle sprint down to the water. They splashed into the waves. Gabrielle, who appeared to love the colour red, wore one of the smallest two-piece bikinis Sarah had ever seen. She was curvy and gorgeous. Sarah pointedly looked away, suddenly feeling inadequate. She knew she had an attractive figure too. Just not as—well, not as voluptuous as Gabrielle.

Gemma had on a teal green one-piece suit with a high front and a racer back that looked like it had been worn by the winning relay team in some nameless competition. Gemma wasn't much for the aesthetics of fashion, always wearing what was comfortable and allowed her to do as she pleased. She had a muscular, athletic build and swam like a fish, which was no surprise. She was good at all sports. Sarah, on the other hand, enjoyed the water, but would never win any races.

She'd better get a move on. Pulling her top over her

head, she revealed the blue and white striped bikini she'd worn underneath. Tossing her shirt aside, she peered around for Raphaël. He had moved several chairs down to carry on an animated conversation with another couple.

Of course, he'd know people here. Sarah slid her skort down to her knees and bent to untie her shoes. He and his girlfriend or wife Gabrielle were probably here every day. She grimaced at the sand.

"I wanted to have time alone with you—to talk." Raphaël's deep voice startled her, and she flew up in surprise.

"Talk?" She kicked off her shoes and reached for her towel, wishing she could fling it over her head and hide. This was awkward. The best she could do was hold it in front of her and adjust her sunglasses.

"Yes," he continued gently. "*Seulement pour une minute.*" He glanced to where Gabrielle and Gemma were just two dark heads against the bright azure waters. Then he turned back to run a hand through his hair.

"I want to apologise for being so rude. I don't think you arranged to stay with my friends at the same time I was 'ere. It was such a shock to see you that I first believed you 'ad some strange motive in organising such a meeting." Raphaël dropped onto the chaise opposite and looked earnestly at her. "I realise I was mistaken." He shrugged. It was a gesture she'd seen him perform so many times she almost smiled in remembrance. But things were different now.

Sarah felt more than the heat of the sun on her face as she stammered a response. "Thank you. I—I truly didn't know who your—your friends were, or that you might be here. I only knew there were people you often visited in Italy. It's truly bizarre that we ran into one another." She attempted and failed at a laugh.

"It is okay," he said, reaching out to pat her hands where they twisted together on her lap. "*Je comprend*s. I understand. I was young also and must shoulder part of the blame for why things didn't work out."

"I appreciate that. I suppose we just weren't meant to be."

A breeze lifted his dark hair as he shuffled forward on the canvas lounger and made a move to rise.

"Shall we swim?" He reached out to her, offering to help her stand, his brown eyes holding hers in a look of forgiveness and friendship that melted her heart.

"Wait Raphaël, I—I need to tell *you* something."

He settled back with a quizzical expression on his face. Sarah shuffled the sand under her feet and then told him in a flood of words, all that she'd wanted to say so long ago once she'd realised what a fool she'd been. "I'm so sorry for hurting you. I behaved like an idiot." She shook her head, trying to rid herself of the unhappy memories that flooded over her. "I was wrong to break things off by sending you a text. It was cowardly and stupid." She looked up. He had gone very still and pale, but she couldn't stop until she'd said it all.

"I have no excuse other than I was young and silly, and so thoughtless. I—I've always regretted what I did and thought many times of calling you to apologise. Now, so many years later, I can only ask your forgiveness." She took a deep breath and looked away, unable to face the hurt that flared in his eyes.

"You 'ad regret?" It was Raphaël's turn to duck his head and stare at his feet. "You regretted the *way* you ended our relationship? Or regretted that you ended it at *all?*" His voice was low and husky as he glanced up, his eyes searching and unfathomable. Sarah had to lean forward to catch what he said and wasn't quite sure if she had heard him correctly. Though before she could ask him to repeat it, Gabrielle ran toward them along the beach.

Reaching them she cried, "What are you waiting for? Come down to the water. It's so refreshing." Laughing, she flicked her braid at Raphaël, spraying him with droplets of water. Pivoting on one bare foot she turned and ran back from where she'd come.

With one last searching look at Sarah, he grinned and stood. "We 'ave been summoned," he said, once again offering to help her up.

"I don't need to be told twice," she said lightly, accepting his hand of friendship. But when his firm hand clasped hers and drew her toward him she found her breath constricting in her chest. She sprang away, afraid he would see how flustered she felt.

Unfortunately, she'd forgotten her skort was hanging around her knees. She pitched forward with a screech. Raphaël attempted to catch her, but it was no use. She tumbled to the ground in an ungainly heap and laid there laughing—feeling like an idiot.

Her cheek rested in sand that already reflected the heat of the sun, only adding to the flush in her cheeks. She closed her eyes and wrestled with the clothing wound about her ankles. Her shout had attracted the attention of neighbours who stood to their feet to see what was happening. Great.

"*Est-ce que tu vas bien?*" Raphaël was on his knees beside her, concern along with laughter etched on his face.

"I'm fine," Sarah muttered, scrambling to her feet. "Thank you."

She leaned over, snagged the offensive clothing, threw it with unnecessary violence at her lounger, and took off for the water at a jog. Not one of her finer moments, for sure.

His question had unsettled her equilibrium. He'd sounded hopeful that she regretted losing what they had begun so long ago. But what did it matter now? He was married or dating the lovely Gabrielle, and she was beginning a career back home. Such questions could not be pondered with any degree of safety.

Unsure where Raphaël was, she waded out until the water was deep enough and plunged beneath a wave thinking it was a metaphor for her life. She was in over her head.

CHAPTER 6

Sarah was the first one out of the water. Her body streamed with rivulets of the Ligurian Sea. Swiftly, she made her way to the lounger, grabbed her towel, and wrapped it around herself. Then, stuffing her clothing into her bag, she made her way purposefully toward a cabin she'd noticed upon entering the beach area. It appeared to house a shower room that she planned to make use of.

After rinsing off, combing through her hair, and applying a little lipstick, she emerged to see the others still frolicking in the waves. That was fine. She'd downloaded a book to her phone and would do some reading. She set her bag in the sand and moved the large umbrella to a better position before settling down with hat and glasses to read.

There hadn't been much free time to relax since they'd arrived in Italy, despite what she'd expected. Sarah was methodical about her teaching and had spent most of her free time studying and preparing lessons. It was a little intimidating to teach adults and particularly ones where there was a language barrier to begin with. It had taken some special training, before she'd been considered a worthwhile applicant and she had wanted to do the best job possible.

But all of that was behind her now. Restlessly she stood up to adjust the angle of the lounger. The last thing she wanted to do was fall asleep and burn. She sat down and tried to read again.

Next thing she knew, a hand was gently shaking her by the shoulder and she opened her eyes with a start.

"You 'ad a good nap?" Raphaël asked with a chuckle.

"Oh!" she sat up so fast she almost knocked the drink he was holding into the sand. "Sorry. I didn't mean to nod off. It was just so warm and relaxing."

His grin deepened, as once again, he offered her a glass and a short bottle of yellowish liquid. It looked a bit like lemonade. She accepted it gratefully, poured it into the tiny glass, and took a sip.

"Ooh." She shook her head with surprise. "That's not lemonade."

"*Non*. It is Crodino, a popular non-alcoholic aperitif in Italy. Refreshing, yet surprisingly different." He held his own up to the light before taking a deep swig straight from the bottle as though performing in a commercial. Then he looked at her, his face a wreath of smiles. He sat and leaned back in the lounger next to her, lifting the bottle again, and signalling they should make a toast. Sarah raised her glass to clink with his.

"To friendship and forgiveness," he said. "I am glad to see you again, Sarah."

"*À votre santé*," she said, recalling the French words

to toast one's good health. "I'm glad to see you again too."

"Must we be so formal?" he asked, staring out to sea as Gemma and Gabrielle walked, toward them dripping.

"You mean, using the word *votre?*" Sarah took another sip. It was cold and revitalising, but she couldn't quite figure out what was in it.

"*Oui.*" Raphaël turned to face her again. "The familiar form of the word 'you' is *tu*. We are more than casual acquaintances, you and me. Yes?" He gave her a mock disapproving look over the rim of his glass.

She nodded vigorously. "Of course. I'd forgotten the informal term." She blushed again, thinking of the closeness he referred to and not wishing to discuss it further. They'd spent every waking minute together during the time she visited his family's estate in France. What beautiful memories they'd shared, but painful ones too. The 'what ifs' of life rose up and threatened to choke her. Blinking rapidly, she pretended to concentrate on reading the ingredient list of the bottle she held.

"Do you think it is time to get some lunch?" Gabrielle came to a stop between them, wringing out her hair, directed a question at Raphaël. "Could we take them to our favourite spot?" She snatched up a pink towel and draped it around her middle before rummaging for her sunglasses in the backpack Raphaël had carried.

He slapped his knees with the palms of his hands and stood. "*Bien sûr*. But of course," he added, glancing at Gemma who busied herself with a brush. "There are showers available to you over there." He pointed to the building designated for women. "I believe Sarah found it already, so we three will get ready and meet back here. *Bien?*"

"Sounds great to me," Gemma said enthusiastically. She grabbed her bag and marched across the sand. Gabrielle and Raphaël followed behind. As they hurried away, side by side, Sarah stared at Raphaël. Despite telling herself not to, she felt a stir of attraction for the man. They had gotten along famously in the past. It had been such fun to discover their mutual enjoyment of skiing and dancing, and their joint dislike of bananas, rap music, and horror movies. And, at each day's end he would kiss her outside her bedroom door. Her heart ached when she remembered being in his arms and the closeness they'd shared.

Considering her age at the time, he'd been such a gentleman, never asking for more than a simple kiss. He had hoped she would stay at his family estate in France to pursue their burgeoning relationship, but thanks to her that hadn't happened.

Sarah shook her head to clear her wayward thoughts. This line of thinking had to stop. She lay back on the recliner and finished her drink. Jagged stone reared from the sea not far from her and the water gently lapped at its base. The rocks of the Cinque Terre were so timeless. For hundreds of years people had been living, loving, and dying along this scenic portion of the Italian Riviera. Considering the history that had already elapsed made her problems seem insignificant. Ultimately, she was happy with her life choices. It was best to put all doubtful thoughts out of her mind and concentrate on living in the minute.

"You seem deep in thought." Gemma plunked herself down at the end of Sarah's lounger and dropped her bag onto the sand. "Anything serious?"

"Nope." Sarah straightened and plastered a bright look on her face. "Just a bit sleepy is all. You had a good swim?"

"Yes. It's so gorgeous here and they're great people to spend time with." She lowered her voice to a conspiratorial whisper. "Now that I've met Raphaël, I'm sorry you didn't stay with him. He's hot, and nice. If he's only dating Gabrielle, maybe it's not too late."

"About that..." Sarah began saying, but bit her tongue as the woman in question appeared at her elbow.

"Shall we go?" Gabrielle asked.

Sarah scrambled up and slung her backpack over one shoulder. "Definitely," she said, hoping none of Gemma's remarks had been overheard.

Somehow she needed to get Gemma alone and stress to her that she did not want to spend another day with these people. It was for the best that Raphaël was with another woman. She could focus on her future back home and put Raphaël out of her mind. Gemma needed to understand that. Her friend wasn't thinking in her usual level-headed manner at all.

Movement caught her eye as Raphaël emerged from the men's changing room and waved, waiting while they gathered their gear and walked toward him.

As they drew alongside, Gabrielle linked arms with him. "This will be fun," she said, looking into his face with pleasure and then back at her two new friends. Raphaël patted her hand indulgently.

The attractive couple led the way out the exit. To

the left was a long promenade that ran along the seafront. A metal fence prevented people from entering the paid beach area, but beyond it stretched rows of umbrellas where holidaymakers reclined in the sun or swam in the tranquil waters. Benches, potted flowers, and trees blooming with red and pink flowers lined the walkway. Across the street, and also to the left, were houses, hotels, and the occasional shop covered in vines or graced with the long overhanging branches of a palm tree.

However, Raphaël led them to the right along the street and then veered into a long brick-lined tunnel cut into the rock. They stayed close to the edge as cars also used this path to access the town.

Soon, they passed under huge arches that supported the train tracks and entered a series of narrow, winding streets. There was no hurry other than their growing hunger. They sauntered along, while Gemma and Sarah revelled in the sights and smells that emitted from each open door.

Restaurants were in full swing as it was almost noon. Tables and chairs spilled onto the street beneath umbrellas and awnings. Each chair was filled with a happy patron, every mouth full and smiling, while the busy clattering of dishes, pots, and pans filled the air.

Washing hung to dry from upstairs windows, motionless in the heat of midday. Flowerboxes, vines, and other assorted greenery also graced the upper windows of the buildings they passed, but every shutter was drawn against the heat.

They passed shops where focaccia bread of all varieties was displayed in a showcase window out front.

The scent of baking bread was divine and Sarah fell back a pace or two just to breathe it in.

Souvenir shops bursting with keychains, commemorative t-shirts, bracelets, and other memorabilia were plentiful. Clothing to be sold hung from racks outside the doors of tiny shops. People strolled in large numbers, making it difficult to walk two abreast in some places. From behind, Sarah watched as men were drawn to the beautiful Gabrielle. A few wives or girlfriends noticed the men's open-mouthed appreciation and yanked them away. Sarah felt plain by comparison to the lovely woman ahead of her. Raphaël was indeed a lucky man.

Then, suddenly their direction changed. They ducked down a tiny lane where few tourists walked and the hubbub died away.

There, beneath an unassuming sign announcing the name of the restaurant, they stopped, and Raphaël motioned they follow him inside.

"*Ciao*, Marco," he said, as a man hurried to greet them. "*Un tavolo per quattro, per favore.*" With a broad grin, the man inclined his head. He was slim. Sarah guessed he was probably in his fifties, with slicked back hair and a thin moustache. He drew wet hands across his apron.

"*Si, si. Da questa parte,*" he said, leading the way through the busy tables to an empty one along the far side.

The temperature dropped about ten degrees inside the building and Sarah pulled off her sunglasses and then her hat to shake free her already dry hair. It felt good. Their server pulled out a chair for each of the women, seating Gemma opposite to Gabrielle and Sarah across from Raphaël. Then he handed them menus and backed away to attend to others who had ventured through his doors.

Sparkling crystal and polished flatware were on the table already and, mainly because the menu was all in Italian, Sarah took a moment to gaze at her surroundings.

The furnishings were made from a dark wood, but the table linens under their plates were spotlessly white. One wall was devoted to wine bottles, floor to ceiling, and they gleamed in the light that filtered through the expansive windows all along the front. There was a standing cooler to one side that held cold drinks and a dazzling array of desserts. Sarah had an impulse to window-shop in front of it. She did love sweets. Somehow, she held herself back.

The back area of the restaurant was in perpetual motion as white jacketed chefs prepared food. The aroma was almost overwhelming. A grill kept a kitchen fan in constant use and the sizzle of meat and fish was mouth-watering. Sarah wasn't used to eating much for lunch, but she was on holiday after all, and it smelled too good to resist.

After they ordered, with Raphaël's assistance, Sarah leaned back in her chair to relax. But Gemma began asking questions and Sarah stiffened. With Gemma's penchant for asking anything that flew into her extroverted head, there was no relaxing to be had.

Without preamble, Gemma began. "So," she said. "How long have you too been together?" Part of Sarah cringed at the boldness of her friend's query and the other part was fearful of the reply. Was he indeed married to the lovely Gabrielle, or only dating?

"Together?" Gabrielle had been busy checking her phone, but now focussed her attention on Gemma with reluctance. "What do you mean, together? We only arrived in Vernazza two days ago. Not long before yourselves."

"No, no..." Gemma giggled. "I mean, how long have you been dating, or are you two married?" She picked up her napkin and smoothed it across her lap as she waited expectantly for her reply.

As understanding flooded her face, Gabrielle looked appalled. "Married!"

Across the table, Raphaël leaned back in his chair, his eyebrows lifting and a broad grin splitting his face in two.

"*Mon Dieu! Raphaël est mon cousin, pas mon mari.*" Gabrielle was so shocked, she lapsed into French. Gemma looked to Raphaël for clarification.

"She said we are not married, nor are we dating." He chuckled. "We're cousins."

Gemma kicked Sarah under the table. "Oh, isn't that interesting," she said with a meaningful glance at Sarah. "And here I thought you two were such a cute couple."

Sarah prevented a screech from leaving her mouth and moved her bruised ankle out of Gemma's reach. Great. She'd hear about this revelation tonight for sure. It didn't matter that Raphaël was still single. There were too many years and hurts between them to go back now.

Raphaël explained. "My mother's brother, Benard, lives in Toulouse with 'is family. You would 'ave met them if you were in France for Julien's wedding." There was the merest suggestion of reproach in his tone and Sarah avoided his gaze. "Gabrielle and Annette are 'is daughters, *mes cousins.*"

"I see," Sarah shrugged. "And you probably knew I was Angelina's cousin." She looked over to Gabrielle who was checking her appearance in a tiny compact mirror.

"*Oui*," she said, turning to Sarah and snapping the lid shut. "I am sorry we did not tell you we were related earlier. For some reason I thought you knew." She smiled. "Angelina is a wonderful woman. 'Ave you met their new baby boy, Philippe?"

Sarah shifted uncomfortably on her chair. All this reminiscing was a little too close for comfort. It swirled around the painful memory of her and Raphaël's breakup. She wondered if Gabrielle knew about that too. Probably.

"I have met the baby, yes. Although, I suppose he's not a baby any longer at two years old." Sarah managed to crack a smile. "Angelina and Julien brought both children to Canada for a visit last Christmas. Celeste will be five now, I suppose. She's such a sweetheart."

Before anything more could be said, the food arrived. Sarah had ordered the *gnocchi con baccalà* with Taggiasca olives, cherry tomato confit, and toasted pine nuts. Raphaël had assured her it was delicious. As the large dish was set before her with a thump, she wondered how she'd ever eat it all. But when the fragrant steam reached her nostrils, she vowed she'd do her best not to leave a single bite behind.

Raphaël's enormous seafood platter was clumped

onto the table, then followed Gabrielle's *L'Acciugata alla Monterossina,* which was an anchovy spaghetti. Gemma watched as a steaming plate of *pansotti* was placed before her. Gabrielle had explained that it was ravioli filled with greens and cheese, and then smothered with a walnut sauce.

Sarah was so busy checking out the wonderful array of dishes on the table that she was the last one to pick up a fork. Raphaël had not been wrong. She lifted a light-as-air morsel of gnocchi into her mouth and closed her eyes in rapture. It was fabulous.

Of course, the added bonus was the topic of conversation changed. After a few bites, they began to discuss the rest of their day.

"We thought we would take you to a wine tasting," said Gabrielle, a tiny dot of tomato sauce on her chin. Long eyelashes fanned across her cheeks as she bent to apply herself to another mouthful.

"Oh, that sounds marvelous," Gemma gushed. "There must be quite a few in the area, is there?"

"The one we enjoy is not too far from 'ere and the experience is well worth the visit." Delicately, Raphaël picked up a shell filled with a gelatinous mound and tipped the contents into his mouth. Sarah averted her eyes. Seafood had never been a favourite of hers and the sight of raw oysters slithering down someone's throat was too much for her to watch.

"I'd love to go, but are you sure it's not altering your plans for the day." Sarah dabbed her mouth with her napkin and reached for the wine Raphaël had ordered with their meal. "You really don't have to spend every moment with us."

"But it 'as been our pleasure," he said graciously. "Perhaps we will walk around the town first though, *n'est-ce pas?* There is the Church of Giovanni Battista, built in the 1200s and the San Francesco Church where a few major artworks are housed, as well as the Statue of the Giant which I would like you to see. It represents Neptune, the Roman god of the sea. We 'ave time since our appointment to taste the wine is not until five."

As he waited for their response, Raphaël studied his glass, swirling the ruby-red liquid thoughtfully like a professional sommelier. Sarah was reminded of the estate he and his brother Julien ran in France which produced both wine and olive oil.

"That would be lovely," she said. "I suppose it's interesting for you to see how other wineries operate.

"It is," he said, taking another mouthful. "And 'ow are your parents?

"They're great. And Elyse? Angelina told me she married Armand. I'm glad for them both."

He rolled his eyes. "*Ma mère va très bien, mais...*they are never 'ome. She travels all the time since 'er marriage to Armand. They are quite a pair. So 'appy," he finished, almost looking wistful.

"She deserves it." Sarah turned to Gemma, feeling as though she were leaving her friend out of the conversation. "I met Elyse, his mother in Canada when I was visiting family in Quebec. I've told you about the holiday I took to France with my cousin Angelina?"

"Mmm, yes," Gemma's mouth was full. "Your estate sounds beautiful," she said, nodding at Raphaël.

"It is!" Gabrielle responded with enthusiasm. "I spent much time there as a child."

The group fell silent to indulge in the delicious meal. Soon, Gabrielle and Gemma pushed their plates away. Gabrielle snapped open her compact to apply a fresh coat of lipstick and dab at the wayward spot of sauce on her face.

Raphaël smiled indulgently at his cousin. He leaned back in his chair and stretched out his legs. Unfortunately, Sarah's legs were there too and they tangled briefly. Her eyes flew up to meet his as he murmured an apology and straightened. Yet, where his bare leg had brushed against her own, her skin still tingled. Sarah dragged her eyes away from Raphaël and turned her attention to the windows, feeling heat creep up her cheeks.

On impulse she decided to do a little shopping, thinking that perhaps a few moments alone would help her to regroup. "I'd love to take home a few souvenirs," she said, downing the remainder of her wine and scraping back her chair. "Perhaps I'll duck out quickly and do that. There was a store nearby."

She stood to her feet hurriedly and almost fell flat on her face as she tripped over Gemma's backpack. Her face grew even hotter. "I'll see everyone in a few minutes," she muttered and rushed to where she'd noticed other people paying. Quickly she used a credit card to cover all four meals and with a brief wave to where they all still sat with their wine, she ducked outside.

The summer heat hit her like a wall. Hoisting her bag over one shoulder, she slid on her sunglasses, and crammed her hat on her head as she strode along the alleyway and burst out onto the main street, joining the throngs of passersby. The shop she'd noticed earlier was just across the busy road and she made for it with a purposeful stride, glad to put some distance between herself and Raphaël.

While she was grateful they'd talked, and she'd had a chance to apologise for the past, she was ready to remove herself from his constant company. She and Gemma needed to get back to the holiday they'd planned for just the two of them. Sarah pushed thoughts of Raphaël away, choosing to ignore and not analyze why they came so frequently now.

Arriving at her destination, she chose a tea towel with a scene of Monterosso al Mare embossed on the front, and a scarf, colourful in shades of blue, yellow, and orange for her mother. Then she found a keychain and a mug for her father, paid for them, and popped them into her bag. They were only small trinkets of the area. She'd gotten her parents, other, less touristy items when she'd shopped in La Spezia.

She began looking through a rack of t-shirts thinking she might get something for herself as well.

"Well, hello there beautiful," said a husky voice in her ear. "Haven't I seen you somewhere before?"

She whirled around, knocking into the stand of clothing. Slowly, it swayed and toppled forward, but leaping into her path, a grinning Raphaël caught it before it hit the pavement. He secured the swaying garments, coming so close she could smell the spicy scent of his cologne. She took a deep breath, battling an urge to run her fingers through the thick, black hair that curled over his ears and brushed his neck. His sultry black eyes held hers for only a moment, and then he moved away.

"*Désolé!*" He bent to look at her closer and rested a hand on her shoulder. "I didn't mean to frighten you."

"You still wear the same cologne," she said softly, lost in a world of memory. She could have laid her hand on his, and very nearly did so before she caught herself with a shiver and stepped back. His eyes locked on hers again, just as they had in the restaurant. He was getting too close and familiar. Remembrances were flooding back and threatening to overwhelm her. She swallowed the lump in her throat.

"Thank you," she said. "It was clumsy of me." She stepped away to make a fuss of straightening the clothes before walking out to the street.

"M*erci beaucoup* for the meal," Raphaël said, following her. "You did not 'ave to pay for ours."

"Of course, I did!" She stopped dead and rounded on him. "You've been so kind to take us with you today and pay for our entrance to the private beach. If you'd have had a choice, I'm sure I wouldn't be your first choice in a companion." She continued walking.

Raphaël looked away and changed the subject. "Did you find the souvenirs you were looking for?"

"I did, thanks. And where are the others?" She craned her neck to see if she could spot them in the crowd.

"We noticed you right away, but Gemma said she was looking for a pair of boots and kept walking. She asked that Gabrielle keep 'er company, so I came to let you know what was 'appening."

"Ahh." Sarah said no more, but easily read between the lines. Her so-called friend was doing her best to create an opportunity for Sarah and Raphaël to be alone.

"Shall we look for them?" she asked, striking out without waiting for his reply.

He fell into step beside her. "What I said was true. You *are* as beautiful as ever, Sarah." She dared a look at him, but his face looked as though it had been carved in rock—impassive and staring straight ahead. He sounded as though he were merely stating a fact, not as though he were interested in a flirtation.

"Me?" She laughed rather scornfully. "Thanks, but you don't have to say that. When you knew me years ago I was a vain young thing, entirely consumed with my appearance. I still am a little, I suppose. Perhaps all women are to some degree, but I've grown up. I now know I'm not all that pretty and I've learned what's really important."

"And what is that?"

"People. Experiences. Love. Acceptance. Not necessarily in that order." She stole another sideways look at him. His profile looked thoughtful.

"That is...profound." He pointed to a shoe store on their left and waited while she crossed in front of him.

Gabrielle leaned against the outside wall of the store, consulting her cell phone, and unconsciously attracting the attention of every man who walked past.

Sarah wove her way through the crowd, past several stands of shoes and stood beside her. Raphaël joined them and an uncomfortable silence fell over the trio. Politely, Gabrielle slipped her phone into her purse and tucked it by her side. Sarah wracked her brain to think of something to say.

"Do you still live in Toulouse?" she finally asked. "I understand it's a beautiful city." Sarah shaded her eyes against the sun as she studied the young woman.

"*Mais non,* I attend the University of Paris-Descartes. I am in my final year working toward a psychology degree and I love it." Her eyes shone.

Sarah was taken aback. She hadn't expected this disclosure. If Gabrielle had revealed she was a fashion designer and modeled bathing suits on a Parisian runway, or had recently become a glamorous young actress, she would not have batted an eye—but to hear that Gabrielle was studying the human psyche was a complete surprise.

"I'm impressed," she said, after taking a moment to digest the news. "That's a challenging field."

"It is, but a most rewarding one. I 'ope to help many people one day." She flicked her thick rope of ebony hair over one shoulder. "*Et toi?*" she asked in return.

"Me?" Sarah answered, her brow furrowing. "I'm an elementary school teacher. Gemma is too. We took the summer off from job-hunting to come to La Spezia and teach English to adults. After our trip, I'll go back to Canada and continue the search for employment." She pushed her sunglasses higher on her face. It was hot, standing in the full sun. She wished Gemma would hurry.

"You are giving back to society and the world as a whole," Raphaël broke in. "I contribute to humanity in another way—through their stomachs." He chuckled at his own joke.

"But that is true," Gabrielle retorted. "Do not laugh. You give the world olive oil to eat which is the healthiest oil known to man, and you give them wine to refresh their spirit and 'elp them to laugh and forget their troubles. It is a worthwhile endeavor." She turned to include Sarah in the discussion.

"I agree," she said simply. "One occupation is no more honourable than another."

"Well, thank you dear ladies." Raphaël bowed with a flourish.

At that moment Gemma appeared, clutching a bag. "Found a pair," she exclaimed. "And at a great price. Sorry for holding you up. Just give me a minute to stuff them into my backpack and we can continue."

As she hefted the bag onto her shoulders, the group moved back into the flow of pedestrian traffic and continued their stroll, interspaced with a little more shopping. After several pleasant hours of rambling, and visiting *Chiesa di Giovanni Battista,* a church built between 1244 and 1307, Raphaël signalled it was time to make their way to the winery.

"It isn't far," he told them. "We simply follow the Via Roma, although it is an uphill climb. May I carry your bags?" He directed his question to both Gemma and Sarah since he was already lugging Gabrielle's things with his own. When both women shook their heads, he shrugged with a smile. "*D'accord.* Let me know if you change your minds."

They passed under arches and walked past colourfully painted homes, more small vendors with tables pushed onto the street, food markets, and clapboard signs advertising both the restaurants and their menu of the day.

The sky was dazzlingly clear and bright. Not a cloud marred the blue perfection above. Eventually they left the main streets behind and entered an area of apartment buildings with satellite dishes perched on every balcony, much like at home.

Within about fifteen minutes, they arrived at the winery's canopied entrance. Raphaël disappeared through the darkened door, then returned, and beckoned them to follow.

Stepping down a few stone steps below street level, they entered a cave-like foyer where every wall was covered with glistening bottles of wine. Soft, ambient lighting lent the space a warm glow. It was filled with round tables, four chairs to each, that were filled with contented guests. Several of the groups were enjoying platters of small appetizers that reposed on the tables in front of them along with, of course, shining goblets of fruity wines.

A long counter stretched across the far end and behind it stood a middle-aged blonde lady beaming from ear-to-ear. She was slim, as so many Italian women were, wore a blue dress, stylish sandals, and her hair was clipped into a bun at the back of her head. She led the way across the room to an empty table where she seated them with a brief explanation. Her English was good, although heavily accented. Sarah found it all quite charming.

"I will bring you five white wines," she said, placing an illustrated paper placemat on the table in front of each one. "They are from each of the five villages of the Cinque Terre. The wines will correspond with the information you see before you." She swept a hand over the descriptive mat in front of Gemma. "If there is one that you like, they are all for sale. I hope you enjoy your visit." She smiled broadly and bustled off to fetch the drinks.

Sarah stared at the paper in front of her. There was a sweet Sciacchetrà that she read was traditional in the Cinque Terre. It sounded the most appealing to her. She wasn't fond of dry wine, but reading further she learned that another wine they would test was a classic dry, aromatic wine characterized by, among other things, 'a delicate bouquet of hay.' That was strange. She'd heard of citrus, oak, or floral elements in wine, but dried grass was a new twist.

The wine arrived. Five glasses were gently placed in front of Sarah, and she sat back to celebrate the moment with her companions.

"Shall we try the same one at the same time?" chirped Gemma, fairly squirming on her seat with excitement.

"I think we should. We will begin on our left and proceed through to the right," Gabrielle said. She must have done this a thousand times before, and even more for Raphaël. Still they joined in the enthusiasm of their guests and lifted the first glass on the list to toast one another.

"Santé," they said in unison and clinked their glasses before taking an experimental sip. Sarah and Gemma swallowed theirs down with gusto, but Sarah noticed Raphaël and Gabrielle performing a short ritual before they took a drink.

First they held the glass aloft and inspected the liquid as they swirled it in the light. Then, they buried their noses in the glass and inhaled. Lastly, they took a small amount into their mouths and almost chewed on it before swallowing. She was entranced.

The pair looked at one another thoughtfully.

"This one is good. It 'as a crisp acidity, wouldn't you agree, Gabrielle?" Raphaël held his glass up to the light again.

"Definitely," she turned her head to one side and nodded. "Yet complex."

Gemma caught Sarah's eye and winked. They had no comments to add when speaking to people with such a wealth of knowledge on the subject of wine. Sarah took another drink and read on her placemat that this particular variety came from Monterosso. She took note of the other visitors in the room who didn't appear to be aficionados either.

"Shall we taste the next one?" asked Raphaël, his gaze resting on Sarah as though her opinion was the only one that mattered. She glanced quickly to the others, observing that Gemma was giving her an I-told-you-so look over the rim of her glass.

"Yes, sure. This first one was delicious," she ventured. "Although I'm not a connoisseur."

"You do not 'ave to be." Raphaël lifted the next glass and squinted at it. "It is about enjoying the experience and sharing a drink with friends."

"I know for sure *I'm* having a great time," said Gemma, with a slight inflection in her voice that let Sarah know she referred to more than just the drinks. Sarah scowled at her friend.

The blonde-haired lady was back at their table in record time bearing three long, rectangular plates of food. She slid them in-between the many glasses.

"*Buon appetito*," she said, before hurrying away.

On one of the white porcelain dishes there was a variety of sliced fruits, oozing syrupy juices. A selection of thinly sliced meats and cheeses reposed on another, and the third contained a number of open-faced sandwiches. Some were draped with thin curls of prosciutto and others were clearly a version of bruschetta. Still more were spread with greens resembling watercress and others with a creamy white mixture drizzled with a sauce made from capers, olives, and tomatoes, among other things. One hardly knew where to start.

"This will be my dinner," announced Gabrielle. "It's all so tempting I know I will be quite stuffed afterward." Grinning at them, she took a plate from a stack that had been placed on the table after the food and began loading it.

"Please, help yourselves," Raphaël urged. He handed Sarah and Gemma each a dish and waited while they selected what they wanted.

"This is so nice," Sarah said. "Thank you for bringing us here." She felt her appreciation rise for this handsome man that sat across from her. He had truly forgiven and forgotten the abysmal way she'd handled their breakup and had treated both her and Gemma to a wonderful outing. His eyes crinkled at their corners as he smiled expansively.

"It is my pleasure," he said.

She sank her teeth into some bruschetta and rolled her eyes. It tasted as good as it looked. The four bantered back and forth, laughing and talking as though they were old friends. Sarah suspected the wine had something to do with that, at least on her part, but she wasn't complaining. Considering the rocky start, it had been a lovely day.

Finally, after finishing every drop of wine and last crumb of food, they sat back in their chairs replete and relaxed.

Sarah glanced at the table next to them. The parents of two disinterested teenagers were enjoying the remainder of their wine while their offspring stared listlessly at cell phones. Sarah smiled to herself and then, with a start, she thought of Tyler and the ridiculous number of times he'd rung her last night.

She hadn't checked her phone in hours. Perhaps someone else had texted, like other friends. Those would be phone calls she'd enjoy receiving. Dragging her backpack out from under the table, she rummaged inside feeling anxious. Flicking it on, she entered her password to find a text from her mother, but no one else. Good. She heaved a sigh of relief.

"Is there a problem?" Raphaël searched her face.

"No," she said. "My mother wrote asking how things were. I'm going to take a picture to send to her. She'd love this place." Sarah aimed her phone at one of the glistening walls of wine bottles and snapped a photo.

"You should bring her here someday."

"On a teacher's salary I'll be lucky if I ever get back here again, but I'd love to show my parents a few of the marvelous sights I've seen." She didn't mention that her parents could have paid for fifty trips to Italy or anywhere else they wanted to go, for that matter. Her family's wealth always made people uncomfortable, so she usually left it out. Sarah motioned that the girls should move close together for a shot.

"Give me your phone," Raphaël instructed. Gemma slung her arm around Gabrielle on one side and Sarah slid her chair over to throw her arm around Gemma's neck on the other. They grinned obligingly as he captured the moment.

"Thanks." She took her phone back. "Do you mind if I take yours?" She had hesitated in asking yet thought he might feel a bit hurt if she didn't.

"*Bien sûr*." He pushed his chair back to face her.

She stared at him through the anonymity of her phone camera. He was such a handsome man. Sarah admired the flash of white teeth in his tanned face, the dark eyes filled with good-humour, and the slight shadow of beard around his strong jawline. She took the picture just before he moved any further and almost knocked over a cart stacked with dirty glasses. Opening his mouth in mock horror, Raphaël lurched out of the way. She snapped another two pictures, noticing how the thin cloth of his cotton shirt tightened over his muscular arms.

Then, as he and the others rose and prepared to leave, she tapped out a short message to her mother, promising to send more pictures of the day when she was back at the B&B. Quickly she grabbed her bag and followed Raphaël to the counter.

"I'd like to pay for my share of this," she whispered. Slanting a look back at Gemma, she noted her friend had no compunction about leaving Raphaël to pay.

"*Mais non*," Raphaël pushed her euros away. "This is

what I wanted to do for you and your friend. It was good, yes?"

"It was wonderful," Sarah said with a heartfelt sigh. She put a hand on his arm to give him a little pat as she would have done with anyone to show her gratitude. Yet with Raphaël it was different. It was as though an electric shock passed from her fingertips throughout her entire body. She looked into his eyes, her shock registering in the slight widening of his. She snatched her hand away, wondering what had just happened. Had he felt it too?

"Thank you," she mumbled, and marched to where the two women stood waiting.

The four of them stepped into the street outside. The sun had slipped behind the mountain, the temperature had cooled, and the crowds dispersed. A couple wandered past, the young woman clinging to her young man's arm with one hand, the other extended in front of her as she ogled a ring in the dying light. They were giggling as they passed. Sarah averted her gaze.

"I suggest we catch the train to Vernazza," Gabrielle said, matching Sarah's lengthy stride. "It 'as been a long day."

Gemma trotted to catch up and linked arms with Sarah. "It has. But a great one."

The trek was all downhill from where they were and before long the group stood on the platform awaiting the train. They didn't need to buy tickets. Fortunately, Gemma had known to have them both purchase a pass for walking the trails in the national park as well as for riding the train. Gabrielle and Raphaël produced their passes too.

A small group of happy visitors shuffled to and fro as they waited, but soon the train whistled into the station and screeched to a halt. People piled aboard. Sarah and her group stood back chatting until almost everyone else had boarded. As she placed her foot on the bottom rung to step up, someone appeared from the side and jostled her sideways.

"Scusa," the man shouted as he pushed ahead of her. Sarah teetered precariously for a moment until she felt a strong hand on her arm steady her. She didn't need to see who it was to know. The now familiar tremor of awareness coursed through her body. Hurriedly, she jumped up the last step into the train and, clutching her bag to her chest, found a seat beside Gemma. Raphaël tossed his backpack onto a rack above his head and fell into the seat across from her.

Staring out the window he remarked. "The distance from Vernazza to Monterosso is a very short train ride, but not so short when one is walking in the heat, *n'est-ce pas?*"

"Not short to walk, no," Sarah smiled. "Yet I wouldn't have missed it. The views were magnificent." She busied herself with scrolling through the many pictures she'd taken of the walk, the beach, and the town.

"What are you guys doing tomorrow?" Gemma queried. Her phone falling to her lap, Sarah rounded on her, her eyes widening in horror, but her friend was the picture of innocence. She tried to surreptitiously elbow Gemma into awareness, but it was no use. The woman was on a mission. She turned to face their new friends with an apologetic smile.

"We aren't going to bother you again tomorrow, are we Gemma?" she said, giving her friend a glare that threw daggers. She plastered a falsely bright smile on her face. "It was a lovely day, but we have plans tomorrow as I'm sure you do too."

Raphaël said nothing. Sarah, stealing a look at the pair sitting across from her from under her lashes, saw that Raphaël's face looked a bit drawn at the prospect of spending another day with them. In spite of that, Gabrielle looked positively thrilled with the idea.

Great. Gemma was cracked in the head to suggest another outing together, but there wasn't a thing Sarah could do about it without looking churlish.

Gabrielle clapped her hands together. "I would love to travel with you both tomorrow. We 'ave no plans, do we Raphaël?"

"*Non*, indeed we do not. It would be our pleasure to join forces once more. If you would like to do so?" His dark eyes sought Sarah's. "Gabrielle and I must leave you in Vernazza tonight, to make your way back to Romeo's B&B on your own. I must speak to a friend before the night is over. But we could meet over *le petit déjeuner* tomorrow morning to discuss our ideas?"

"Of course," Sarah said, struggling to look excited. "That would be nice."

One of Raphaël's eyebrows raised at the word 'nice' and a half smile crossed his face. He knew she wasn't thrilled with the idea, and she could tell he wasn't either, but they'd both been backed into a corner.

"*Bien*, then it is settled," he said. "And just in time, as we 'ave arrived at the train station in Vernazza." He stood as they came to a stop and reached for his bag.

"You will be alright to climb the hill this time?" He grinned at Sarah, teasing her. "You 'ave no massive metal *valise* to carry now."

She giggled in spite of herself. "Thanks for your heartfelt concern." She jabbed at his arm as they walked down the aisle. "I think I can scramble back to the B&B without being carried."

They stood together on the platform as passengers surged past them to get on the train for Corniglia, the third village in the string of tiny gems along the northern stretch of Italy's coastline.

"Until tomorrow then." Raphaël ducked his head, speaking to them both, but outright staring at Sarah. His gaze softened. "*Bonne nuit* to you both."

Sarah didn't trust herself to speak. She nodded to both Gabrielle and Raphaël, and then turned to walk away.

"Yes, good night you two," Gemma called. She looked smug as she caught up to Sarah and fairly danced in front of her once they were out of earshot.

"I got us another invitation," she fist-pumped the air. "Aren't you glad?"

Sarah stopped. "No. I am not glad. You are interfering and exasperating. I'm really cross with you right now. All day you've been pushing me at him, and I'd like to know why?" She folded her hands across her chest and waited for Gemma's response.

Even in the gathering dusk Sarah noticed Gemma's face took on a stony obstinacy.

"I think you two should be together," she said with a sniff. "Maybe you just don't realise it." Her voice turned sulky. "I guess you don't appreciate what I'm doing, but I *am* trying to help you."

"You're right. I don't appreciate you meddling in my love life, and I want you to stop. You did the same thing with Tyler, constantly harping at me to break up with him. You don't know what's best for me, Gemma. We'll go with them tomorrow because you forced it to happen, but after that you won't push anymore...Okay?"

Gemma was silent as she strode along the Azure Trail that led to their temporary home.

"I said—okay? Did you hear me?" Sarah was losing her patience.

"Yes," came the irritable reply. "I get it."

They completed the hike back to Luna and Romeo's in silence. Though as they quietly climbed the stairs to their rooms, Gemma paused and suddenly sat on the steps, blocking the way. She rested her head in her hands and looked pleading.

"Please don't be mad anymore. I really was only thinking of you, but I'll stop interfering from here on out. It'll be just you and me again. Forgive me?" Gemma manufactured such a look of wretched remorse that Sarah laughed.

"Alright. I forgive you. Just remember what I said," she finished sternly.

But as Sarah reclined against the lavender scented pillows after a shower and sent the pictures she'd taken that day to her mother, she wondered who she should be angry with. Her finger unconsciously traced Raphaël's smiling face on the screen. She gave herself a shake. Turning off her phone, she set it on the nightstand and clicked off the light. The situation was becoming complicated. She ruined her chance to be with this man five years ago and didn't want to risk hurting him again. She must make every effort to avoid the debonair Raphaël and his cousin. It was the only way.

She lay in the darkness, trying not to think of the smiling dark-haired man who intruded on her dreams.

CHAPTER 7

Sarah drew back the curtains in her pretty room and looked toward the shimmering sea. Her phone told her it was only 7:30 a.m., but the sun had already scaled the pale blue sky behind the guest house to cast its glow on the Cinque Terre.

She reached for the handle and pushed the door wide, stepping onto the balcony to delight in her surroundings, forgetting she shared the space with whoever had the room opposite hers along this west side of the house. Once at the railing, she rested her hands on the top rung and drew in a deep breath of contentment.

"*Bonjour*," said a deep voice.

Dammit! Sarah whirled around, feeling exposed. She hadn't thought to get dressed first and only wore a gauzy nightgown that hugged her curves.

Raphaël sat at one of two circular tables on the long deck, a laptop opened in front of him and a coffee cup nearby. He was dressed in a white, short sleeved, button-up and, below a pair of knee-length jean shorts, his long brown legs were crossed at the ankle and jutted out from beneath the table where he worked. He looked brooding and thoughtful.

"Hi." Crossing her arms across her chest she moved away from the railing and hurried back to her door. She managed a brief smile in his direction before she ducked inside the sanctuary of her room. Pulling the heavy drapes over the glass, she walked into the bathroom, feeling ill at ease. A whole day spent with this man was going to be challenging.

Might as well get ready and try to make the best of it. She squeezed toothpaste onto her toothbrush and leaned over the sink. Actually, yesterday had been a lot of fun. It was just...well, she got the distinct feeling that Raphaël had forgiven her for the past. Except he went back and forth between wanting to like her again and trying to keep her at arm's length. She could tell he wasn't keen on spending time together. That was fair, she reasoned, but made things a little awkward. Her stomach clenched as she went about her preparations for the day.

After rinsing her mouth and washing her face, she hung the washcloth to dry and stared at her reflection. The frown lines on her forehead were getting more pronounced. Maybe she should have just gone home. If she had, none of this would have happened.

She sighed and put a foot on the edge of the bathtub to smear a liberal dose of sunscreen onto each leg, followed by her arms and neck. She applied her usual makeup, a touch of lip gloss, brushed her hair into a high ponytail, and moved to the wardrobe where she'd hung her clothes.

She rifled through the large selection of clothes she'd brought, finally choosing a short, white, eyelet-lace dress with gathering at her midriff. A long scalloped ruffle pulled low off her shoulders, skimming her creamy-white arms on top, and ending light as a cloud just above her knees. She moved back to the mirror, tipping her head to one side as she studied the dress' effect. The ruching at her waist was attractive, showing off her fit arms and legs. It looked nice on her slightly leaner, but still hourglass figure, she decided. Not on par with Gabrielle, perhaps, but it would do. She fastened a delicate necklace with a gold heart around her neck, grabbed her hat and backpack with all the essentials, and hurried to the landing. She paused. No noise emanated from the other three doors, so she assumed her companions were already downstairs.

They were at the breakfast bar. When Gabrielle saw her she set her plate down and rushed to Sarah, grasping her shoulders, and kissing both cheeks. The young woman looked stunning in a deep coral dress with a bright green and yellow tropical print. A wide-brimmed hat with matching material wrapped above the brim lay on the table.

"*Bonjour*, Sarah. I am so glad you are 'ere early. We will get a good start on the day." She pulled away with a wide smile.

"*Bonjour*." Sarah grinned back. She really liked this young woman with her infectious laugh and outgoing demeanour. "I'm not so late today."

"*Non, pas du tout.* It is good." She looked pointedly at

Gemma as she returned to her dish and stepped back to the bar to spear some fresh fruit. "I should say it in English, sorry. I am not sure if you know any French?"

"I don't," Gemma agreed. "Well not much anyway. But French is a beautiful language and I enjoy hearing it." She seated herself in the same spot as yesterday. "I picked up some Italian while I've been here, but not enough to use more than polite words." Gemma wasn't waiting for anyone else to join her. She cut into a crusty roll and lavishly spread it with strawberry jam. As always, Gemma looked cute, but ready for a day on the trails in her tan-coloured cargo capris, hiking boots, and a simple, blue and white striped t-shirt. Her standard green ball cap was hooked over her chair along with her other gear.

"Per'aps you will visit us in France sometime." Raphaël clumped his dish onto the table and stepped across the room to accept two tiny porcelain cups of coffee from Luna who had appeared around the doorway with one in each hand. The lady nodded to the group and disappeared.

He set one of the frothy drinks in front of Gabrielle and motioned to Sarah with the other. "This one is for you." He winked solemnly as he set it at her place and turned on his heel to stride into the kitchen. "Yours is next," he called over his shoulder to Gemma.

Sarah's eyes followed Raphaël as she walked around the table to sit down. How kind he was. A vision of her visit to his family's estate in Provence flashed in her mind. He had always been thinking of others and finding some small service he could perform to surprise them.

She shook her head as Gemma snapped her fingers under her nose. "Hey! Wake up! Gabrielle just asked us what we'd like to do today."

Gabrielle was frowning at Gemma when Sarah looked up with an apology on her lips, but the girl quickly schooled her features back to normal.

"Sorry Gabrielle. I wasn't paying attention. I think we're open to whatever you suggest."

"*Pas de problème.*" Gabrielle waved Sarah's apologies away. "I 'ave an idea. It would be nice for you to see the Cinque Terre from the water. So, I was thinking we could catch the ferry from Vernazza to Riomaggiore and do a little exploring along the way. You could get some wonderful pictures."

Raphaël returned with more coffee and added to the conversation. "The ferry leaves every three hours." He consulted a gold watch on his arm. "If we are at the dock in fifty minutes we can enjoy a leisurely trip to Riomaggiore, with an alternate view of the coastline. Then, we could spend some time visiting the castle, the church of San Giovanni Battista, eating, drinking, and sampling gelato before we take the train back to Manarola to watch a golden sunset reflected on the colourful stone houses. For our grand finale, we'd catch another train to Vernazza. What do you think?" He looked quizzically at them all.

"I think you should have been a travel writer," Sarah said dryly. "Or a stage actor."

With a grin, he waved a theatrical hand and lowered his head to take a bow.

She fought the urge to stare and focused instead on her pastry and coffee. "I'd love to go."

Gemma ceased to chew as she propped her head on a hand, listening to the wondrous plan Raphaël had shared. "It sounds fabulous."

"*Bien*. It is settled." He reached for his cup.

After it all, Sarah couldn't help herself and looked up. Raphaël's eyes were filled with mirth as he caught her gaze. What a change from the angry man that had sat across from her only yesterday. Her heart gave a little flip, and she averted her eyes. Even though it spelled trouble, she liked this version of Raphaël much better. Perhaps a little too much.

※

It hadn't taken long for them to finish breakfast and scurry down the path into Vernazza. They walked single file up the gangway, presented their tickets, and stepped onto the boat. Sarah was becoming quite used to the raspy sound of the cicadas in the trees by now and knew she would miss it, the sunlight sparkling on the Ligurian Sea, the stone terraces curling up the hillside, and the vineyards and olive trees they contained. It was truly breathtaking. No wonder Raphaël came back every year.

Sarah followed her friends onto the boat and edged along the row to a plastic seat beside Gabrielle. She and Gemma both shrugged off their backpacks and tucked them under the seats. Raphaël, who had stood as the women settled themselves, now slid into place beside Sarah. She was intensely aware of him, but he made no attempt to be closer. After a few moments she relaxed and prepared for the voyage. She loved the water. The gentle rocking motion of the craft filled her with anticipation. Soon, they were loaded, the plank was tucked away, and the engine fired up.

Raphaël was right. Riding in the ferry lent a whole new perspective to the coast. Craggy cliffs of bare rock reared from the sea while scraggly, wind-blown trees clung to the stone anywhere they found purchase. Occasionally she spotted the train as it flew between the towns and a few times it was possible to see the tiny figures of hikers winding their way along the rugged paths. Her phone was getting crammed full of the fabulous pictures she was taking.

They passed Corniglia first. The houses were perched, higgledy-piggledy, high on the hilltop, one hundred metres above the sea.

"From the water, it is the least accessible village of the five, as there is no port," Raphaël told her above the wind. "But there are walking trails that link it to the others, and of course, the train."

"It's beautiful. Everything here is exceptional."

"Next to my 'ome in Provence, it's my favourite place on earth. I try to come at least once a year."

Surreptitiously, Sarah gazed at his profile. The breeze ruffled his dark hair and caused his shirt to billow in the back, pulling it taut against his lean chest. Sarah tore her eyes away, giving herself some stern advice.

You are not dating this man and are not allowed to be attracted to him. You're not allowed to entertain fantastical ideas. You are going home to be an elementary teacher and live a quiet, uneventful life. Now smarten up!

But even as she finished berating herself, the

thought of returning home caused a knot to grow inside of her. She looked across at Gemma and was surprised to see that, rather than watching the gorgeous scenery fly past, Gemma was observing *her* with a strange half-smile. Her friend's hand lifted briefly in a thumbs-up signal before she placed one arm on the side of the boat and stared over the water.

Sarah wasn't going to waste time thinking about what it meant. Since the moment they'd arrived, Gemma had been pushing her into Raphaël's arms. How far would her friend take this foolish notion?

Gabrielle, who must have made the trip many times, sat between them, scrolling through messages on her phone. "The terraced hillsides are so interesting. I never tire of this journey, but..." she said, trailing off and shrugging absently, "my boyfriend is also important."

"What's his name? Does he go to university with you?" Sarah asked.

"*Il s'appelle Lyam, et no,*" she smiled wistfully. "*Mon copain est guide touristique à Paris.*" She laughed and corrected herself. "Sorry for the French. My boyfriend is Lyam and 'e works as a tourist guide in Paris." She waved her phone in the air. "I miss 'im, but we will be together soon. Do either of you 'ave anyone waiting for you at 'ome?"

Gemma leaped in before Sarah could even formulate a thought. "No." she declared. "I haven't seriously dated for a couple of years...and Sarah broke up with her boyfriend long ago."

Sarah stared at Gemma over Gabrielle's bowed head. "Long ago?' she mouthed.

"Oh?" Raphaël spoke quietly, his foot beginning to

tap a rapid beat on the floor of the boat. "You were seeing someone, Sarah? Was it serious?"

Gabrielle's fingers paused momentarily on her phone. She swivelled around to listen to Sarah's answer.

Sarah looked at Raphaël, but his face was set in hard lines, like granite. The muscles of his neck tightened as he waited for her answer. "It was—" she began, but before she could finish the word let alone the sentence, Gemma leapt to her feet with a screech of amazement.

"Do you see that?" She lunged to the edge of the boat and leaned dangerously far over the railing, jabbing her finger at something no one else could see. Her feet came off the floor of the boat and waved in the air as she slid forward over the verge.

"Gemma! Sit down or you'll fall in," Sarah cried, but it was too late. Their craft bounded over the waves of a passing speedboat, causing all of the seated occupants to bounce in their seats. Gemma slipped sideways. She yelped, glided over the side, and toppled headlong into the foamy water with a resounding splash before disappearing from view.

Sarah blinked owlishly, frozen in place.

The ferry continued on its merry way not knowing anything had happened. Sarah and Gabrielle came to life, leaped to their feet, and screamed as did many others. The engine was killed.

"Man overboard!" someone hollered, after the fact. Most of the passengers had already jumped to their feet. The captain hollered at them to sit down. Raphaël rushed to the back of the ferry, kicking his shoes off as he went. In one smooth move, he put a foot on a vacant seat to boost himself and dove into the churning waters.

Sarah fought her way through people who had stood up and moved into the aisle to see what was going on.

"Gemma! Gemma!" she shouted into the wind.

But her friend was lost in the swirling waves that surrounded the large boat. Nothing could be seen in the frothy water behind them. She gripped the railing with white knuckles, in danger of falling over the side herself.

Did Raphaël spot Gemma? Sarah couldn't. She couldn't even glimpse Raphaël in the frothy water. Rising to her tiptoes, she strained to see. She knew she wasn't a good enough swimmer to save someone's life, so she'd stayed put and watched as Raphaël's dark head bobbed into view and his powerful arms sliced through the surf.

Gemma was like a frog, Sarah told herself, frantically scanning the water. Unless she'd been knocked unconscious, or caught in the propellers, she knew her friend was strong enough to swim back to shore two times over. She'd won gold medals for long-distance swimming at university. Heck, she'd worked as the coach of a swim team three evenings a week back home and was a lifeguard on the weekends to make extra money for school.

Sarah, Gabrielle, and the rest of the commuters anxiously skimmed the surface of the water. Someone threw two life preservers into the fray as well, but they bobbed uselessly beside the boat.

Then suddenly, Sarah spotted a second head when Raphaël was only a few metres away. He had her. Sarah whirled around to grab Gabrielle in a hug.

"She's okay." Sarah's voice caught in a sob and her legs felt weak. She turned to the railing and clung to it until Raphaël, with an ashen-faced Gemma, reached the side of the boat. She helped pull her chum inside.

Gemma collapsed in a puddle onto the deck and Sarah fell to her knees beside her.

"Are you alright? What happened? What was out there that was so flippin' exciting you had to jump in after it?" Sarah felt like crying with both relief and anger, an aftermath from the fear that had gripped her heart.

"Just get me back to my seat, and I'll explain," Gemma croaked. She was a sodden mess—her clothes stuck to her and water streamed down her face. Grasping her hands, Sarah hauled her friend upright amid cheers from the crowd. Someone threw a towel around Gemma's shoulders as she limped back to a chair and flung herself into it. She huddled there, shivering miserably.

Raphaël, who'd also been given a towel, was receiving congratulatory pats on the back as he made his way back to their row of seats and plunked himself down against the side of the boat as though to prevent any further mishaps. He lifted a hand, motioning all was well to the captain of the boat. The engine roared to life and they continued their journey.

It took a few minutes for the general hubbub to settle down. Raphaël mopped his face and scrubbed at his hair with the bright red towel before taking it back to its owner and collecting his shoes. Sarah watched him as if in a dream. What had just happened? Within the space of about ten minutes, a catastrophic event had taken place during which her dear friend could have died.

Whatever would possess the woman to lean so far over the edge of the boat?

"I've made a fantastic fool of myself, haven't I?" Gemma moaned, burying her face in the towel.

"Accidents 'appen," Gabrielle said comfortingly. "We're all just glad you are back on the ferry with us."

"The sun will dry me off now." Gemma handed the towel to Sarah with brimming eyes. "Did you see where this came from, and uh, could you please return it?"

Sarah marched the towel back to its owner with much thanks. The older lady and her husband spoke rapidly in German. Despite being unable to understand one another, with hand gestures and smiling, the message of gratitude was conveyed.

"So, what in the world did you see that caused you to leap up?" Sarah asked, plunking herself beside Gemma and lowering her voice. Raphaël and Gabrielle were talking amongst themselves. Sarah knew she sounded accusatory and tried to calm herself.

"A killer whale. Or maybe a shark. I—I dunno." Gemma looked thoughtful, avoiding Sarah's eyes. She pulled her t-shirt away from her body and wrung out the end. "I lost my favorite hat," she moaned, feeling the top of her head. "And my sunglasses too." She slumped even further down on her seat.

Sarah felt irritation clutch her insides again for what could have happened.

"Wait a moment." She clenched and unclenched her hands. "I need a better explanation than that. Are you telling me you think you saw a killer whale, that by definition kills things? Or perhaps a hungry, man-eating shark? And what...You decided to fling yourself into the water to get a better look? Fancied a little up-close-and-personal time, did you?" Sarah's voice rose with sarcasm and incredulity, attracting looks from the people around her. She lowered it to a hoarse whisper. "Are you completely crazy?"

"Not completely crazy. Just partially." Gemma had the grace to look sheepish although she still tried to make a weak joke about the whole incident. "It all happened so fast. I know it was foolish to stand up and lean over the side like that. I guess I wasn't thinking. When we hit that wave I just flew up and out. What else can I say?"

Sarah flopped against the back of the seat, lifting an arm to her brow, and feeling worn out. Closing her eyes, she took a deep cleansing breath and looked her friend in the eye. "I apologise for getting upset. I was scared." Sarah put an arm around her friend and drew her close. "I'm so glad you're okay."

"You don't need to apologise. I was a stupid idiot." Gemma squeezed her hand and then leaned forward to direct her next words at Raphaël. "Thank you so much for rescuing me." She gave him a wobbly smile. "You're a wonderful swimmer."

"You are most welcome, although I do not think you needed my 'elp." He shrugged expressively. "I am just 'appy you are safe." He ran a hand through his wet, tangled hair and looked off to their left as the next village came into view. "There is Manarola. It is not far to our destination now."

He was doing his best to take the focus off what had just happened and bring the day back to normal. Sarah was grateful. She looked in the direction he pointed and saw the tiny village coming into view.

"Umm, Sarah?" Gemma whispered, looking at her friend with an apologetic expression. She pointed at her knee. It was swollen and turning a nasty shade of purple. Standing up experimentally, she tried to put weight on it. "Ouch!" She collapsed back. "I'm not hiking anywhere today." She glanced at the hilltop village.

Leaning close to Sarah, Gemma continued to speak quietly. "I think when the ferry docks, I'll get off and take the train back to Vernazza." She held up a hand of protest when Sarah opened her mouth to argue. "I know you'd stay with me, and personally see me back to the B&B, but I don't want that. I've already caused enough trouble today and…I…I…" Gemma stopped and twisted the end of her wet t-shirt around her hand again, clearly agitated. "I need to tell you something. This morning, I decided I'm not going back with you to Canada just yet. So, that means I'll have the time to see these things. I want you to go on without me."

"What?" Sarah blinked. Was she floating in a perpetual fog today? "You've decided not to go home? For how long? Why didn't you tell me before this?"

"I only changed my plane reservation this morning. There was nothing to tell before that. Anyway, the point is, I'm staying in Italy for another two weeks and you aren't. I want you to enjoy yourself." She grinned at Sarah. "I'm going to go see Venice and Florence while I'm still here. Who knows? Maybe I'll stay in Italy forever, just like in the movies." She shrugged. "Anyway, for sure I can't walk very far. Must have banged my knee on the railing when I went over." Wincing, she stretched the leg out in front of her. It really did look painful.

Sarah felt dazed. "But what about the time we were going to spend together? Why didn't you tell me before it was all settled? We had plans." She shook her head to clear the fog. "What about Rome? I don't get it Gemma." She felt tears pricking her eyes, but blinked them away as she waited for answers. When they didn't come, she continued.

"Fine then. I'll get off *with* you and we'll both return to the B&B. You'll need help to climb the trail. Raphaël and Gabrielle can keep going. We'll meet up with them later because I'm not leaving you alone, especially when you're hurt."

"No," Gemma spoke sharply. "I said, I want you to enjoy yourself." She enunciated slowly. "You only have one more day in the Cinque Terre after this. Go." She flipped her hand as though brushing Sarah off. "Have fun."

Gabrielle interrupted by moving into their space and slicing an arm through the air between the two women. "*I* will stay with Gemma," she announced. "I 'ave ridden the ferry, walked the trails, and seen every village many times before. I come 'ere with Raphaël almost every summer. It would be nice to just sit in the shade, enjoy a drink with Gemma, and call my Lyam," she explained with an exaggerated wink.

"Is that alright with you, Sarah? Would you be opposed to spending the day with just me?" Raphaël joined the conversation, frowning as though preparing to be turned down. Sarah couldn't do that to him. Not again.

"Of course not," she said with forced brightness. "It's a wonderful idea. I just feel bad dividing our group is all. And with Gemma hurt..." She swung back to her friend. "Let's stay in touch through texts, okay? And if you need me, just write."

"It only takes a few minutes for us to get back by train if she needs you," he said. "We will not be far away."

"Okay," Sarah said reluctantly.

Gemma appeared satisfied and swung on her backpack. "We'll be fine."

The ferry chugged through the water on a course to dock. When it stopped, passengers crowded forward to exit the craft while those waiting to board shifted restlessly on a small shelf of pavement built into the rocks. Gemma hobbled behind the other people, leaning heavily on Gabrielle's arm. They paused to wave and then were lost in the crowd of folks surging forward.

The ferry pulled away continuing onto the next leg of the voyage to Riomaggiore.

As the wind once again offered respite from the heat, the noise of the craft and its passengers rose. Sarah spoke to Raphaël.

"*Merci beaucoup* for acting so quickly to save Gemma." She tucked an errant strand of hair behind her ear. "I don't understand how it happened, but I'm grateful for what you did." She looked into his face, so close to her own. Her breath seemed to catch in her throat. His mouth turned up at the corners creating a dimple in his left cheek that she remembered well. The urge to cover the short distance between them and touch her lips to his became so strong that she swayed, and then moved back, wondering how she was going to get through the day. It must be her heightened emotions over Gemma's fall that had her feeling so rattled.

"Are you alright?" Raphaël laid his hand over Sarah's hands where they twisted together on her lap.

She flinched, but didn't pull away. It felt so...good. She turned her head to meet his gaze. His eyes radiated warmth. Almost as though his compassion was seeping from *him* and into *her*. A strange calmness washed over her and she sat, mesmerized in the glow of his concern.

And then, her phone dinged, and she came to her senses. What was she thinking? She snatched her hands away and dragged her backpack from its resting place to rummage in its depths.

"*Désolé mademoiselle.*" Raphaël lifted both hands in the air as she yanked away. The friendliness of his face had shut off as though a switch had been flipped.

She noticed the change and sadness washed over her, but perhaps it was for the best. He was getting entirely too close, and she feared what might happen. They had to get through one day together, as friends, without her hurting him by leaving again.

Dragging her cell phone from its waterproof pocket, she unlocked it and almost keeled over when she saw who it was from. Tyler. She checked the time. It wasn't even five in the morning there. Why in the world would he be writing her at this hour? It was so out of character that she immediately read the note, worried that something dreadful had happened to her parents.

'I miss you.'

Relief mingled with irritation washed over her. Sliding the phone back in its case, she dropped it into her bag. There was no way she was responding to him, ever again. She zipped her bag, and held it primly on her lap, almost as a shield.

Although Tyler was becoming increasingly strange, he was the least of her worries. Raphaël was undermining her defenses, just by being his wonderful self. She couldn't allow that to happen. Not when they were to spend the entire day in one of the most romantic places on earth.

Alone.

CHAPTER 8

As they approached Riomaggiore, the fifth village of the Cinque Terre, Sarah saw the train burst from a tunnel and shoot across a trestle bridge spanning a valley before vanishing into another hidden cave within the rock on the opposite side. A cluster of pastel-hued houses appeared, hanging precariously from the rocks. Nestled together along the center of another valley, they spread up both banks.

This tiny village was as quaint and as pretty as the other four, while maintaining its own unique charm. The ferry docked and a temporary metal bridge slid forth to span the gap between the rocky shore and the boat. Smaller craft, along with colourful kayaks, bobbed in the water nearby, moored along a jumble of boulders in the petite harbour.

Raphaël stepped aside, allowing Sarah to leave first. He brought up the rear after sharing a few words in Italian with the captain of the vessel. Sarah was sure that the poor fellow had been unnerved by the events of their voyage. Doubtless there weren't many passengers who pitched headlong off the ferry during his normal workday.

Sarah trailed behind other people who were visiting the town. When they were clear of the gangway, she stopped and waited for Raphaël to decide on their next move.

"Are you still quite soggy?" she asked, as he walked up to her.

"Not in this 'eat." Raphaël was always upbeat. "It's actually quite refreshing to be a little damp." He appeared quite unfazed by his precipitous dip into the Ligurian Sea. "Although I might fancy something light to eat and per'aps a drink. What about you?"

"I'd love it." She adjusted the pale green day bag that hung from her shoulder.

"Have you had any of Ligurian focaccia?" When Sarah shook her head, he continued. "It is the best in all of Italy. What do you say?"

"I say it sounds *perfetto.*" Suddenly she felt as light-hearted as she had at nineteen years old and first getting to know this man. Her head told her to back away, to be cold and aloof, but her heart...well, that was a different matter. It was only one day, after all. What could happen in a few hours?

His face creased in a smile. "*Bien*. A perfect choice for lunch, and I know exactly where to go." He offered her his arm. Sliding her hand into the crook, and walking side by side, somehow felt right. They ascended stone steps and strolled up the narrow lane past the harbour. Winding his way knowledgeably through the busy streets, filled with tourists and vendors, he led her up several narrow staircases cut from the rock itself. Towering houses appeared to be stacked one on top of another up the steep slopes on either side of the main street.

They ducked into passageways and turned corners until they'd reached a tiny business with a swinging sign over the doorway. He stepped back to allow her to enter first. She paused at the door to view the showcase window brimming with enormous slabs of bread, each one flavoured differently, but all dimpled with the familiar holes that were indicative of focaccia. Some were strewn with rosemary and cherry tomatoes. Others were studded with black olives that shone darkly from the crust like embedded jewels. There were onions, meats, and a host of other toppings too. How would she ever decide?

There were only a couple of tables inside the dimly lit establishment. Sarah moved to the counter to stand beside Raphaël as he ordered them a selection of the flatbreads along with two bottles of fizzy water. A pleasant woman behind the counter slipped each slice into separate, white bags which Raphaël then entrusted to Sarah's safekeeping. He paid, grabbed the waters, and they left.

Raphaël retraced their steps, finding a bench where they could sit in the shade, enjoy the food, and people-watch. He unwrapped the first square and handed it to her.

"Mmm, delicious." She chewed rapturously. "I'm a sucker for a good olive though." She peeped at him feeling coquettish, young and at peace with the world.

They enjoyed their lunch until a large lady in a tight,

patterned dress with a tiny dog on a long leash, puffed up the inclined street and made straight for them.

"*Per favore*," she said, looking meaningfully at the other half of the bench.

Raphaël nodded politely and shuffled closer to Sarah who looked on with a certain amount of shock as first the dog was given prime space, and then the lady plopped down in the middle of their seat next to Raphaël. Between the dog and the lady, more than half of the bench was taken.

Raphaël's leg touched Sarah's and then, as the lady wiggled back and forth to settle herself on the seat more comfortably, Raphaël was shoved up against Sarah so tightly that there wasn't room for her to move her arms. She was pinned to the iron armrest like she was wearing a straitjacket.

Sarah giggled. She tried valiantly to suppress it, but the laughter would not be denied. Holding a stiffened hand over her mouth, she snorted and forced herself to look away. Raphaël squirmed. Without looking at him, she sensed he was fighting the same battle. With effort, he wriggled his arms free and lifted one to slide it around her shoulders, drawing her away from the armrest that cut into her side and giving them both more room. Not much, but enough that they could finish their impromptu meal.

Sarah's giggles had subsided as she felt the familiar ease with Raphaël's body moulded to hers. Her whole being tingled and she had an irrepressible urge to lay her head on his shoulder. Perhaps even snuggle in closer.

But those were crazy thoughts. She tore another hunk of bread from the wrapper and chewed furiously.

Staring at the cobblestones under her feet, she willed herself to pay no notice of those treacherous notions.

Crumpling the bags in her hand, Sarah lifted her water and washed down the last of the delectable bread. It had been a treat, but she was stuffed. She looked forward to walking some of it off.

"So, you're the leader. What's next?" she said, as they struggled with some difficulty to their feet, since they were welded together on the bench. "And I hope it involves some form of exercise because clearly my hips are widening as we speak."

"Yes," he replied absently, looking up the street.

"Yes we're going to exert ourselves or yes, my hips are getting wider?" she asked with a grin.

It took him a moment to catch up with what she was saying. "No, no," he stressed loudly, looking aghast. "Your hips are perfect." He rolled his eyes, flashing her an answering smile. "Silly girl. I do know of a hike we could take." He assessed her footwear. "However, it is a little gruelling," he admitted.

"What is it?" Sarah followed his eyes to her feet. "These sandals are sturdier than they appear."

"It is *Santuario di Nostra Signora di Montenero*, or in English, Our Lady of Montenero." He paused to let the name sink in a moment and then continued. "It is a church, and as far as I know, it dates back to 1335, but that date only reflects the first written account of it. Many say it is much older, possibly from the eighth century."

He turned and pointed vaguely up and to the right. "It is reached by hiking along a circular trail roughly 3.5 kilometres long. Shall we go?"

"Cool." Sarah swung her backpack over her shoulders and held the straps with both hands. "I'm ready for anything you throw at me."

"Excellent." Raphaël looked pleased. "I shall be your tour guide once more. Do you remember all the places we visited in Provence?"

Sarah nodded her head, not trusting herself to say anything. Reminders of their past togetherness was like knives thrust into her heart, at present. The more time she spent with Raphaël, the more she realised what she'd given up. The two of them were well suited and she enjoyed his company immensely.

"Before we go, I want to walk into a *negozio di alimentary*." He looked at her quizzically. "Do you understand what I just said?"

"I'm hoping it's not a brick wall, or heavy traffic." She smirked at him.

He laughed, his eyes crinkling at the corners. She swallowed a lump in her throat as he turned to walk away and called over his shoulder. "Wait for me 'ere, *s'il te plaît*. I won't be long." He disappeared into a store with the word *Enoteca* painted over the door.

What I should have done was wait for him five years ago. Her heart hurt with the thought. She kicked at a loose pebble under her foot. We could have been happy. She paced back and forth as she watched him step out of the *Enoteca* and immediately disappear into a little food store next door. *But no, I was too stupid to do that. I wanted to 'have fun.' Consequently, I ruined the best thing that had ever happened to me.*

Sarah gave herself a mental shake. She shouldn't be daydreaming about Raphaël in any capacity, but was saved from further recriminations by his reappearance. She pushed all thoughts aside, bringing her attention back to the present. He stopped in front of her, his backpack looking bigger and more full. She poked at it.

"Hey, what do you think you are doing?" he demanded in mock anger, rotating away. "Leave a man to 'is secrets."

"You've got something in there. What is it?" Laughing, she pursued him until he grasped her wrists and brought her up against him, their faces so close she could feel his breath. His eyes searched hers for a long moment before dropping to her mouth.

"Okay," she croaked. "You can let me go. I'm not curious anymore." With slow deliberation he did so. Only, his fingers lingered against her skin, caressing her flesh as he released her, his eyes never leaving hers.

"I think we should walk," she said, retreating. Her voice broke and she forced herself to look away. Unconsciously, she rubbed her wrists. That had been a big mistake.

"Did I 'urt you?" At once he was contrite. "I am so sorry, my dear Sarah." He made a move as though he was going to pick her hands up again to inspect the damage he had done to her delicate skin, only she stepped back abruptly.

"I'm fine," she lied with a smile. "Lead on noble sir." She waved at him dismissively. When he appeared mollified, and turned to thread his way through the crowd, her legs almost gave out on her. What was she thinking? This had to stop.

Side by side, they walked through the village. It was larger than she had first thought when they arrived on the ferry. The houses were four and five stories high, each was painted warm shades of orange, yellow, cream, and some were even bright reds and blues. Ubiquitous washing was strung from window to window in some places, while flower boxes filled with geraniums gushed from others.

Soon they left Riomaggiore behind and followed a path that was enclosed on either side by stone walls. Vegetation was thick. Vines crept along the top and trailed over the sides, winding up the trunks of trees whose branches swept over the path offering passing bits of shade.

"What are these trees?" Sarah broke the silence.

"Mostly oak and chestnut," Raphaël answered, glancing over his shoulder. "It is a scenic hike. Are you enjoying it so far?"

"Very much." And she meant it.

The mountainous hillsides rose around them. Terraced vineyards were everywhere in the Cinque Terre and Sarah drank it all in as they climbed at an easy pace. Occasionally there was a door cut into the rock walls that framed the path and Sarah wondered where it could have led. What a fabulous place to live.

Under their feet, stones were embedded in the earth, some pushed up and uneven, disturbed by the unruly roots of trees. In other places steps had been cut from the rock. It certainly kept a person alert, but it wasn't a difficult ascent. Raphaël didn't say much, apart from occasionally enquiring how she was getting on. There wasn't room for two people to walk abreast and that suited her fine. They were simply two old friends out for a hike.

The climbing became steeper as they left behind the framework of rock walls. Sometimes there was a guardrail if the path had a sharp drop-off. Thankfully, they met no one, leaving them alone in a wilderness of green. Sarah was surprised at how few tourists were walking up here. It was quiet and beautiful. She could see the Ligurian Sea glittering in the distance, the sleepy little village beneath them, and vineyards all around. And still they rose higher with every step.

Then, finally they arrived. Sarah followed Raphaël up the path that had become little more than a dirt track into a churchyard that graced the peak of the mountain. The view was breathtaking. Cement pillars were set all around the front of the creamy-white building, skirting the edge of the cliff, and threaded with metal poles to keep visitors safe from falling. A bell tower rose high above the structure and umbrella pines stood in a row, sturdily guarding the side that faced the sea. Crouching, she tried to take pictures that captured the sense of history she felt.

"It is a place where special Masses and religious ceremonies are still held at least three times per year." Raphaël stopped at the front of the sanctuary, staring at the huge arches that graced the front entrance and overlooked the dazzling sea below. "The Virgin Mary was said to have appeared to a shepherd who led her to this place. It was well-known that a den of thieves resided here at the time making it a dangerous spot." Linking his hands together he continued as though reading from a history book.

"The story goes on that, due to this experience with Mary, the bandits gave up their lives of crime and were converted, building a chapel on the spot where she had met with them. Soon, pilgrims arrived, and still do to this day. Eventually the original church was extended. The bell tower still operates. It is beautiful, yes?"

"Oh, yes," Sarah breathed. "Especially after hearing the story. I love it." She tilted her head and allowed a slight breeze to fan her face as she looked over the cliff toward the water. Slowly, she became aware that Raphaël had moved closer. "Can we sit awhile?"

"That was my plan." He dipped his head, gesturing toward a bench at the very edge of the precipice, bordered all the way around by the protective fence. "After you."

The sun slid overhead and beat on them mercilessly. Sarah adjusted her hat against it and seated herself on the hard wooden plank with a sigh. She felt as though she could see to the ends of the Earth from here. Fishing out her phone she took several photos feeling as though no picture could ever do the scene justice.

On either side of them were the rugged hills of the Cinque Terre. Green vegetation covered them resembling a badly laid carpet that folded over itself leaving rumpled gullies, rolling mounds, and dark, shadowy hollows.

Below and to the right, the village of Riomaggiore shimmered in the heat like a set of brightly coloured children's blocks all piled on one another. Just beyond and further along the uneven coastline, other villages clustered—dots of colour over the deep blue of the Ligurian Sea. Sarah clasped her hands together and just looked in awe. It was a vision she would remember always.

She was aware that Raphaël was rummaging in his backpack, but she paid him no mind until he nudged her arm with what felt like the cool rim of a cup.

"Here," he said. "I brought us something to celebrate with." He held two plastic cups half full of what looked like apple juice, but she knew better than that. "Not having a proper glass is almost sacrilegious, but..." he shrugged, and added, "sometimes the choices are limited."

"*Merci.*" Accepting one, she peered into its depths as she had seen him and Gabrielle do at the tasting. She wondered if it was dry, and her mouth puckered at the mere thought.

"It is Sciacchetrà," he said, as though reading her mind. "I know you aren't fond of dry wines, and you like sweet desserts. So, this covers everything. It is a *passito*, a dessert wine with an aromatic taste."

She stared at him over the rim as she sniffed the contents of her glass. How incredibly thoughtful, and amazing that he'd remembered.

"I won't bore you with too many details, but the winegrower hangs the grape bunches in a dark, dry place where they are left to dry for roughly fifty days. This concentrates the flavour and creates a sweetness without becoming syrupy."

She lifted her cup to meet his. "*Santé.*"

"*A l'amour perdu,*" he said cryptically. They touched the glasses together and sipped the wine, their eyes meeting over the rim.

"What does that mean?" she asked, worried she shouldn't ask.

"To lost love." He looked over the railing at the sea

and they sat in silence for a few minutes. Sarah didn't know how to respond and twisted her hands on her lap.

"Are you 'appy?" Raphaël took another sip from his glass and stared straight ahead.

"At this moment, I am—content."

He nodded. "You will return 'ome to—to teach young children now. Is that what you always wanted to do?"

Sarah sensed he wanted to ask her whether she was seeing anyone, but had skirted around the question. Was it because he felt it was not his business, or because he wouldn't want to hear the answer?

"I've always wanted to be a teacher, yes," she pulled off her hat and used it to fan her face. "I haven't found full-time employment yet, though. A permanent teaching position is not easy to secure."

"You will find it. And you will be an excellent educator." His voice took on a different tone, one she couldn't make out. "I am proud of what you 'ave done with your life."

"Thank you." Silence marked the next few minutes. "And you?" she finally asked.

"Me?"

"Are *you* happy?" She reached down to loosen her sandals, kicking them away to luxuriate in the feel of the stony path beneath her feet.

"I am—content," he said, mimicking her earlier response. He twisted his head around to look at her with a twinkle in his eyes. "I would not trade my life in Provence for any other. Producing olive oil and *rosé* wine is my passion. Yes, it was anticipated that I would stand beside my brother and take my father's place on the estate...some might find that expectation a burden. But I would not 'ave it any other way." He reached for the bottle of local wine from within the bag propped at his feet and topped off her glass.

"Naturally, I would like to be married one day and 'ave a family, but that will 'appen when the time is right."

She shifted uncomfortably again and he reached out to take her free hand where it rested on her lap. Twining his fingers through hers he rubbed a thumb across her palm.

"I am not wanting to make you feel bad," he said. "The timing was not right for us before. I understand that now." Releasing her, he lifted his bag onto his knees. "I 'ave something else. But first, why don't we move to a patch of grass around the corner of the building? It will be more comfortable than this 'ard seat."

A weight lifted from Sarah's chest. He didn't hold it against her anymore. She knew he'd said he had forgiven her the day before, but this felt so genuine. It was liberating. Perhaps she *had* been meant to meet him here, in this beautiful place, if only to clear up the painful memories of the past. Now, she could move on with her life minus the guilt.

In answer, she stood to her feet, stretched, picked up her bag, and followed him along the path to where the church provided not only green grass, but shade from the pines as well. Surprised, she watched as Raphaël drew a rolled-up cloth from his bag of tricks, shook it out, and spread it for them to sit on. He motioned that she be seated first then he dropped beside her.

Handing her a clear plastic box from his backpack, he waited while she replaced her hat before pressing a second container into her hands. She held the first up for inspection.

"Fruit," she said in amazement. "How lovely."

"And *le chocolat*." He chuckled. "It would be a grave error on my part if I did not offer chocolate along with the wine."

His face lit up as she laughed with delight and tugged at each lid. Inside one was fragrant, red strawberries, and squares of smooth dark chocolate filled the other. She laid the open cartons on the blanket between them while Raphaël refreshed their drinks.

"A feast fit for a queen, my lady," he joked, lowering his head with mock acquiescence.

"*Merci beaucoup*, Raphaël." She giggled, feeling like a teenager again. "You truly understand the needs of royalty such as myself." Sarah popped a strawberry into her mouth and bit down on the juicy fruit. Closing her eyes, she moaned with delight. What a treat.

They chatted as they ate, sipped the wine, and enjoyed the tranquility of the day.

"You said you were teaching English in La Spezia?"

"To adults, yes. I took a required course on it before I applied for the job, and of course being a teacher already made me a better candidate."

"Yet you didn't meet an 'andsome Italian man while you and Gemma were there?" He lifted his eyebrows quizzically and reached for some chocolate. "I am surprised."

Sarah laughed. "The people that took the classes were mostly business professionals intent on improving their chances of moving up the corporate ladder. They weren't there to meet fresh-faced Canadian girls with stars in their eyes."

Raphaël looked truly puzzled now. "Stars in your eyes. What does this phrase mean?"

"It means we were dazzled by living for two months in Italy and being paid for the privilege. We couldn't believe our good fortune." She sank back onto her elbows and watched an older couple walk past them, purposely avoiding his question concerning Italian men.

But Raphaël wasn't about to let her off the hook. He hit his forehead as though recollecting something important and smirked at her. "I just remembered. You 'ave eyes only for French men. *C'est vrai?*" He pretended to twirl a non-existent moustache and assume a debonair expression. Unfortunately, it looked more as if he were experiencing a nasty attack of indigestion.

"*C'est vrai*," she agreed with a chuckle. "It's true."

She sobered and changed the subject.

"And what's new in your life?" she asked before taking another sip of wine. She watched his face as he concentrated on a smooth pebble he'd picked up from the grass, turning it over and over in his hand.

"Nothing changes. The seasons come and go. We work. Some years the wine is better than others, or the olives produce an 'arvest that is not so abundant, but that is the way of life and farming. We constantly try to improve our operation."

She ran a hand over the short, dry grass beside her and asked the question she'd been thinking all day. "You haven't met anyone special?"

He took so long to answer that she wondered if he'd

even heard her, but finally he tossed the stone back to the path and responded.

"I 'ave dated a few women, yes. None of them came close to you." He drained the last of the wine from his cup and crushed it in his hand before tossing it back into the bag. "There is no one in my life at the moment, if that is what you're wondering."

He didn't ask her the same question. Although she found herself holding her breath, waiting for it. They fell silent, sharing the last two squares of chocolate.

As it melted on her tongue, Sarah's phone beeped. She slid it from the zippered pocket where she'd stowed it and entered her password.

"It's from Gemma," she said after a moment. "She says they're fine and not to worry about joining them till late tonight. Apparently, they're going out for dinner with someone they met in Vernazza. We're to text when we arrive."

Sarah swivelled around to look at him, feeling a little lightheaded from the wine. "Is that alright with you? It wasn't part of your plan for the day. Maybe you'd like to head back as well? To visit with your friends, Luna and Romeo?"

Raphaël busied himself with stashing the snack containers into his bag. Methodically, he zipped it up and set it beside him on the blanket. In a nonchalant voice, he said, "Tell them to do it. I would like nothing better than to spend the remainder of my day with the most beautiful woman I know." Looking perfectly serious, he continued, "Tell Gemma we will be in touch later. After sunset. Not before." He stretched his legs straight out in front of him and laid back using one arm as a cushion. His eyes drifted shut.

Sarah's face went hot. He was joking of course, as she most certainly *wasn't* beautiful. She remembered being quite vain when they'd dated five years ago, but she'd come a long way since then. Life and a few harsh realities had disabused her of those ideas. Tyler had often told her she was attractive in a down-home sort of way, but not really pretty. Why would Tyler lie to her? It was the truth.

Opening her phone again, she typed out the message, sent it, and turned the sound down to low. Gemma was in all probability, contriving to leave her alone with Raphaël as long as possible. Though she didn't care anymore. She was having a good day. Messages from home would only serve to complicate it.

Then, she too laid back on the blanket, modestly tucking her dress in around her. It didn't matter what passersby might think of them lounging on the lawn near a church. Life, at this moment, was perfect. She would worry about getting a job and having to leave this idyllic place tomorrow. Today she was with the man, quite literally, of her dreams.

CHAPTER 9

It had taken them about an hour and a half to walk the path each way. They'd spent another two or three on the hillside enjoying the views and talking. Sarah fumbled for her phone to check the time when they reached the village and began to stroll along Via Colombo. It was almost seven. The afternoon had flown by.

"I want you to see the sunset from Riomaggiore," Raphaël said, stepping along beside her. Occasionally their arms brushed together, sending a tingle down her spine. "It is spectacular."

"I'd like that."

The town was not so populated with tourists as it had been earlier, but still bustling with life and activity. Shops displaying hats, jewelry, clothing, trinkets, artwork, and souvenirs on racks outside their doors, or hanging from hooks on the exterior walls, did a roaring trade as sightseers wandered the streets in droves.

It was a pretty place, with trees almost seeming to

sprout directly from the sidewalk. Pots, overflowing with shrubbery and flowers, also beautified the street that appeared to be pedestrian only, as so many were in the Cinque Terre villages.

"The sun will set just after eight. I think we should 'ave something to eat. Are you 'ungry?"

"I'm not starving or anything. The focaccia still lingers." Sarah patted her stomach. "However, I'd never say no to dinner at one of the restaurants you know, because those are the best."

"I 'ave spent much time in this place, yes." Without warning, he caught her by the hand and swerved between two large groups of people, pulling her close behind him. Laughing, she had to jog to keep up.

Once clear of the crowds, Raphaël slowed, but didn't relinquish her hand. Rather he threaded their fingers together as he led her up a flight of curving stone steps. Sarah didn't pull away, but was conscious of the warmth and comfort his grip evoked. Another set of stairs followed, and then they traversed a narrow alleyway between towering houses.

It was cool in this shaded passageway and felt good after the heat of the afternoon. Moments later, they rounded a corner and Sarah could see where they were headed. A small group of people waited outside the door ahead of them.

"Restaurants, as I'm sure you know by now, do not stay open all day as they do in North America. We tend to 'ave our meals in the evening, particularly in countries where it is 'ot." They took their spot in the queue behind a chattering group of Italians to wait.

Sarah looked up, marvelling at the edifice before

her. The building was made entirely from stone; some flat, formed an arch over the doorway, and larger ones created the impressive wall. A soft light issued from within. Somehow, wonderful smells had escaped around the door, tantalizing her senses. A spindly cactus stood solidly to one side of the entry in an earthenware pot and on the other, in a similar pot, was a small, flowering shrub covered in fuchsia-coloured flowers.

There were sounds of a bolt being drawn back, the heavy wooden door was flung aside, and the throng surged forward. As she stepped inside Sarah felt a thrill of excitement. It was a marvelous place. The rock continued overhead in a sweeping arc, starting at the floor on the right and continuing overhead until it met the floor on the left. It felt as though they were entering a cave, but it wasn't dark. On the contrary, the place glowed with recessed lighting that ran along the floor and was hidden behind a narrow shelf that lined the walls with the roof on either side.

The bar and kitchen were straight ahead behind three square openings at the far end of a long seating area filled with rectangular tables set in an orderly fashion. Every single one was covered in white linens and set with crystal goblets and shining silverware. Even the furniture was white which lent a clean brightness to the space. Sarah was enchanted.

They were met by a pretty young woman in a tight black dress and unbelievably high, pink stilettoes who led them to a table for two near the bar. Handing them each a menu, she lingered over their table, lighting a candle and smiling for such a long time at Raphaël that Sarah chuckled to herself. He appeared oblivious, however. After a moment, the girl moved away with a miffed expression on her face.

"It is nice in 'ere, yes?" Raphaël leaned across the table to speak in a low voice. "I used to be friends with the owners. They were my parents' age and one of the 'appiest couples I knew. Unfortunately, they were killed in a motor accident two years ago. The restaurant changed 'ands since there was no family to take over." He gave one of his expressive shrugs and looked around thoughtfully. "I 'aven't been back since, but I see the present owners 'ave changed nothing. That pleases me."

"It's beautiful," she said simply. "I'm so glad you brought me here. And I'm sorry about your friends. A truly happy marriage seems rare, from what I've seen."

"Perhaps." Raphaël propped his elbows, clasped his hands together, and leaned his chin on them, staring at her. "It is vital to find the right person to begin the journey with. You 'ave not found such a person either?"

Sarah hid her face behind the menu card. Had she? For a time, she'd thought she had with Raphaël, but she was too young to know the difference. Then, at times, when she and Tyler had gotten along, she'd thought he might be the one. But in the end she'd known their relationship was shallow and fleeting. There was no substance or depth to what she and Tyler shared. Eyes downcast, thinking only of the mess she'd recently gone through with him, she answered.

"No," she said, looking up to meet Raphaël's eyes. Yet she looked straight through him. "I haven't met that person," she said tonelessly.

As she spoke, it was as though a shutter came down over Raphaël's face. Too late, she shook herself awake from her reverie and realised he thought she was referring to him.

"Raphaël..." she started to say, but he interrupted her.

"Please, there is no need to explain." He twisted in his chair, searching for the server. "I believe we need some wine while we choose our meals."

"But I want to explain." She laid down the card and fiddled with her fork. "I—I wasn't...I—I didn't mean you. I was referring to someone else. It's complicated and..." Again he stopped her, this time with a raised hand.

"You are not required to expound upon your statement. I knew 'ow you felt about me the first time, *d'accord?* We shall leave the subject alone and enjoy the rest of our evening, *n'est-ce pas?*" His smile was strained and his eyes wounded as he looked again for the server who by this time was almost to their table.

Sarah didn't know what else to do. He clearly didn't want to hear what she had to say. Maybe it was for the best. She didn't want to tell him she'd been thinking about her ex-boyfriend, or who he was anyway. It would be a long and unpleasant story. She stared across the table at him as he ordered a bottle of wine. This man was so dear to her. It might have worked between them if she hadn't messed it up. With a sigh of resignation, she picked up her menu and scanned the items, finding it hard to concentrate.

Inwardly she cringed. It bothered her that Raphaël had the wrong idea. Her heart was heavy. She had to find a way to explain what she'd really meant, without hurting him further.

"Have you decided, *signorina?*" The server was back at the table with their wine and spoke in almost perfect English. As she poured, her eyes flicked up to rest on Sarah's face with bored-to-death disinterest.

"Yes, I have. I mean...I think so." Sarah stumbled over her words. She didn't like feeling so flustered.

Raphaël nodded encouragement. "Do you need 'elp with translation?"

"No...Yes. Ugh, I'll have *farfalle Cinque Terre*." She sat back, pleased that she'd ordered using her best Italian, which wasn't all that great. Yet the girl appeared to understand and wrote it down on her notepad before turning to Raphaël.

"*Tres bien*," he murmured, some of his former good cheer returning as he winked at Sarah. "And I will take the *salmone con finocchio*." He extended his menu card.

Their server sniffed. "*Grazie*." The girl snatched up their menus and marched away.

Sarah chuckled. "She was smitten with you."

"What? That girl? No." He frowned and shook his head, then looked at her curiously. "What exactly is 'smitten?'"

"I'll bet you get hit on a lot." Sarah continued as though he hadn't spoken. She found it an uncomfortable topic of discussion, but once started she couldn't leave it alone. "You're an attractive man. '*Hot*' to quote Gemma when she first saw you."

"Oh?" Raphaël rubbed the back of his neck and flushed.

"Women must throw themselves at you all the time." She leaned back in her chair and laid the linen napkin across her lap. "I know I did. But all that attention has never gone to your head, which is to your credit. You didn't even notice our server."

She was playing with fire, but couldn't resist.

"You *threw* yourself at me?" He leaned forward. Now it was her turn to be under the spotlight. "Tell me more, *s'il te plait*. I find this revelation quite intriguing."

"Well, yes...I suppose I did. Although I likely shouldn't have revealed that." She gave him a lopsided grin and reached for her glass. Her cheeks were reddening again, darn it. "I haven't drunk this much wine in a day since I visited your estate." She licked her lips. "Mmm, this is delicious though. What is it?" Her attempt to change the subject didn't work.

"It is a white wine produced near Riomaggiore, but that is not important right now. I want to 'ear more of this *throwing* you speak of. You believe me to be 'andsome? Irresistible, per'aps?" His eyebrows raised. He was laughing at her now.

"Yes. Of course, I found you irresistible. Surely you knew that." She fussed with her napkin and then straightened. "Look, I'm sorry I brought it up...okay. Let's drop it." The evening was not going the way she had anticipated.

He laughed outright. "You are like the wind, *ma chérie*. You blow one way and then another. Before I can catch up you are off again."

"Sorry."

"There is nothing to apologise for. We will change the topic of conversation." He clasped his hands together and leaned his chin on them. "Tell me, did Gemma say who this person they met in Vernazza was?"

The sick feeling in Sarah's stomach lifted. "No."

"Per'aps she met someone she likes," he said thoughtfully. "We will soon find out." He tipped his wine glass back and forth in the soft yellow lighting and studied the wine. "And when do you fly 'ome to Canada?"

"Tomorrow is my last day here. I head to La Spezia in the evening, pack the rest of my belongings, and the next day, catch an early train to Rome." Tears sprang to her eyes, and she brushed them away. She would not cry, not now. The evening was just taking an up-turn. She wanted this one, last, perfect evening with Raphaël before she left this place. "Gemma and I were supposed to be travelling together. We were planning to spend the rest of that day in Rome, plus one more before flying from Fiumicino."

"I see," he said, his voice quiet. "Well," he gave her a resigned look, before he continued, "we must make the most of tonight...I think our dinner is on its way." He gestured with a sideways tilt of his head.

Sure enough, the young server paced toward them bearing two loaded plates of steaming food. She clunked one down in front of Sarah and then deposited Raphaël's before wishing them an irritated, "*Buon appetito*" and teetering back to the kitchen on her dangerously high heels.

They looked at one another and laughed. Sarah's heart grew wings as she lost herself in Raphaël's enigmatic eyes.

"Shall we eat?" he said, bringing her back to reality.

"Oh! Of course. It smells divine." She picked up her fork and dove in.

Back home no one would dream of ordering a meal

that featured anchovies, but here, in the Cinque Terre, it was a delicacy not to be missed. She'd been told to try them by one of the other teachers at the school in La Spezia before she and Gemma had left for their short holiday. When she'd seen them offered on the menu, she knew exactly what she should order.

The base of the dish was butterfly pasta that had been sautéed with grilled eggplant, sundried tomatoes, capers, olives, and basil before being draped with white anchovy fillets. It looked wonderful, but before she dug in, she peered at the plate resting before Raphaël.

His was a little less unusual in that it was salmon. However, the preparation appeared delectable.

"What is the sauce?" she asked, sniffing appreciatively as her mouth watered.

"Would you like to taste?" Raphaël broke off a few flakes of the fish and swiped it in the sauce and puree before holding it out to her. Again, he sounded like a tour guide as he told her the ingredients. "The salmon is smothered in a lemon caper sauce, featuring a side dish of grilled tomato on fennel puree with spinach."

"Uh huh," she murmured, opening her mouth like a baby bird. He held a hand underneath to prevent drips as he slid the morsel into her mouth and she closed her lips around it, eyes fluttering shut.

"Oh, that's fabulous. Here, try mine." She did the same for him, ensuring every taste sensation was represented on the fork before carefully conveying it into his waiting mouth. His eyes were riveted on hers.

She leaned back, waiting for his approval and knowing they had just shared an intensely sensual moment. He savoured the mouthful. She fancied his already dark eyes had darkened with desire. Sarah had a sudden urge to stand up, take the two steps necessary to reach him and kiss those beautiful lips of his. But she didn't. Instead, she sat with a blissful smile on her face and imagined it.

※

Dusk was gathering. Their meal had been outstanding, but there was no time to linger over it. Raphaël was worried they would miss the sunset. And so, they left the hidden restaurant, retraced their steps down the stairs, made a few quick turns, and reappeared on the Via Colombo.

Raphaël had made no attempt to take her hand again and Sarah was relieved. She was leaving soon; nothing could come of this closeness. She had callously broken up with him once before, five years ago. He would not trust her to not hurt him again, she was sure of it. Besides, her thoughtless words from earlier had damaged the fragile bond that had begun to grow between them. Nonetheless, she missed the warm comfort of his hand.

They strolled with the ease and camaraderie of two old friends. Silent, but comfortably so. When they drew closer to the small harbour, Raphaël spoke.

"Because the village was constructed in a ravine, and due to the height of the buildings, we cannot see the sun unless we are next to the sea where the ferry docked earlier. We could climb up higher, but I prefer to be near the water. Come."

He held out his hand and she needed no urging.

Unquestioning, she took his offered palm and he squeezed hers tight. As if in a dream she followed him along the narrow walkway out to the pier. Was it the wine that played havoc with her senses? She didn't know and didn't care. All that mattered was each golden moment she spent with him.

Words were unnecessary. As they walked, he pulled her closer until they moved as one to the spot he had chosen as their lookout. Strangely, they were alone. With all the multitudes of people that had filled the town earlier that day, it seemed unreal that they two should be so favoured.

Raphaël stopped. Mesmerized, Sarah watched the burning orb slip quietly down to drown in the Ligurian Sea. The fire of its final rays fanned along the crest of the water, lighting it with an orange flame that leapt into the low-hanging clouds on the horizon. It spread like liquid gold along the rippling waves. Shimmering like molten lava and bathing the houses in a ginger glow of light as though reluctant to leave.

Sarah sucked in a breath and held it as tears sprang to her eyes. The moment was etched in her memory. She turned to Raphaël to thank him, to breathe words of gratitude not only for the experience, but for his understanding, his kindness, and for the incomparable day.

But he lifted a gentle finger and laid it against her lips to still her words. His right hand pulled away from hers only to join his left in sliding up both of her bare arms. His fingertips traced the line of her shoulders and neck to finally entwine themselves in her hair to pull the ponytail from its clasp. As her flaxen hair tumbled about her shoulders he bent and touched her lips with his.

It was not enough. His hands moved to the small of her back, moulding her to his body as the kiss deepened. She melted against him. She'd never known anything like this rush of emotion that flooded over her. Not even when she had known Raphaël before. She gave herself up to the sensations it caused. Her arms stole about his waist, her hands splayed out on his shoulders, feeling the hard muscle of his back. His lips moved against hers. Soft and gentle became demanding and a soft groan escaped his lips.

They stood there for what felt like an age, but finally he pulled away. She sagged and stumbled, but Raphaël caught her and they clung to one another again.

The sky, saturated with hues of tangerine and pink, moved to shades of blue and purple as the sun slipped below the horizon. The Cinque Terre prepared to sleep.

"Ahh, *mon lapin*," Raphaël murmured. She moved to lean against him, and he stroked her hair, murmuring the words that only lovers speak.

And then Sarah noticed the moon. It rose in a sliver of luminous white behind the jumble of houses that was Riomaggiore. In its glow she lifted a hand to Raphaël's face, tracing the rugged line of his jaw and turning his face slightly to see what she saw.

"*La lune*," he whispered into her ear. "A full moon inspires emotions and desires between a woman and a man...bringing them into the light."

As he spoke, the radiant orb rose higher in the sky until it hung above the town, bathing it and them, in its silvery radiance. Sarah felt for his hand. He brought it to his lips before gently pulling her back into his embrace. At their feet, the sea rolled tumultuously into the harbour, echoing the beat of their hearts.

And then her phone beeped. It was barely audible, but in the silence surrounding them, the sound was intrusive. It shattered the idyllic dream they had constructed. She tried to muffle the insistent sound with her arm. But it refused to stop. On and on it went until Raphaël pulled away and motioned that she should answer it. Sarah's breath was ragged, her heart beating a tempestuous rhythm in her chest as she ripped open the zipper of her bag and reached for her phone. What she really wanted to do was hurl it into the sea.

"Hello!" she rasped.

Gemma's voice was like a nail going through her brain.

"Hey, where are you guys? We've been trying to reach you! Don't tell me you left. We came to Riomaggiore looking for you and we're headed to the pier 'cause you said Raphaël wanted to show you the sunset. I have a *huge* surprise." Gemma sounded breathless and excited.

Sarah passed a hand across her forehead and pushed a long ringlet of stray hair from her face. It immediately flopped back. "No. We're still here." Putting a hand on one hip, Sarah swayed back and forth. Gemma and Gabrielle were here? In Riomaggiore? Her shoulders slumped.

She looked at Raphaël, a bewildered frown apparent on his face even in the limited light. He bent down to catch her eye. Reaching out he caught the coil of golden hair and tucked it behind her ear, his gentle fingers trailing across the softness of her cheek. She closed her eyes and tried to concentrate on what Gemma was loudly saying. She didn't want to talk on the phone. She wanted to be in this man's arms.

He shoved his hands into his pockets and watched her as she held the phone away from her ear. Gemma's voice boomed from the phone loud enough for them both to hear.

"Okay." Gemma's voice was brisk and business-like. "We'll be there in two minutes. Bye."

"Wait!" Sarah dragged her mind back to the present and what Gemma was blabbering about. "What do you mean you have a big surprise?"

"Not big—HUGE." Gemma paused for dramatic effect. Sarah felt her irritation mount.

"Gemma, just tell me what's going on."

A long, drawn-out sigh preceded her next words. "You're ruining the surprise, but alright. We're only a few steps away anyhow. It's gonna be hard for you to believe this, but Tyler rolled into town. Tyler! On a train. He insisted we come find you."

Gemma's tone became even more strident if that were possible. "He says he's come to propose marriage and won't take no for an answer."

CHAPTER 10

Sarah's heart stopped. Instantly she felt sick and her hands went clammy. Tyler here? Not now. What in the world was he doing? If he'd wanted to harass her he knew she'd be home in a few days. She wrung her hands together and then brought them up to cup her cheeks, scanning the shore and the street leading down to the tiny harbour.

What would Raphaël think? She fumbled for a lipstick in her bag, so that it didn't look like she'd just spent the last fifteen minutes kissing.

She didn't want to cope with Tyler and another ridiculous marriage proposal. Whatever would possess him to come all this way when she'd clearly told him she wasn't even remotely interested? It was a mess of epic proportions. She found the tube and smeared lip gloss across her mouth.

Whirling around, she reached out for Raphaël. He must be told—warned—something! But it was too late to explain. She could see that he had heard the news and turned away, his back to her.

She heard her name called in three different voices, over and over like the tolling of a death knell. Raphaël swivelled back to look at her, his eyes narrowed and hard. She shook her head, lifting her hands in a gesture of hopelessness. She didn't know what to do. She couldn't explain this crazy situation away in the five seconds she had before the trio pounced on them.

Her stomach twisted as she turned and saw the group approaching in the light of the streetlamps. She didn't want to be trapped on this narrow stretch of the pier. Almost jogging, she hurried to meet them, trying vainly to erase the look of dread that she knew was on her face. But it was too far. Tyler met her halfway to the shore.

"This is unbelievable." She sounded desperately unhappy and cleared her throat. He strode toward her, his handsome face looking part thundercloud, part hopeful little boy. A shock of hair fell forward over one eye. She recognized the long, brown cargo pants, lightweight grey sweater, and loafers. She'd helped him pick them out. He pulled at the neckline, looking hot and bothered. It was too warm for such heavy clothes.

Reaching her, Tyler dropped his backpack to the ground and swept Sarah into his arms, lifting her off her feet and burying his face in her hair. "I can't believe I had to hunt you down, sweetheart. I thought you'd be with Gemma, not some guy." He set her down, his eyes narrowing to slits as they focused on a spot beyond her where Raphaël had stopped.

"Tyler, I'd like you to meet Raphaël Belliveau. Raphaël, this is Tyler Morris. He's ...well, he's..."

"I'm her boyfriend," Tyler cut in, giving her an arrogant sideways look. "Nice to meet you. Gemma says you're the guy Sarah was dating before she met me, right? Guess the best man won."

With a sick feeling of horror, Sarah looked back at Raphaël's face. It was tight and withdrawn. He did not deign to answer that question, but turned instead to Gabrielle.

"I think we should leave these people alone, don't you?" Sidling past Sarah without looking at her, or Tyler, he said curtly, "We'll head back to Vernazza. Nice to meet you." Then, he took Gabrielle by the arm and ushered her away.

"Bye," she called over her shoulder. Sarah couldn't see her face in the gloom, but was pretty confident Gabrielle was looking shocked and confused. She was forced to trot in order to keep up with Raphaël's long strides. "Hope I see you tomorrow morning at the B&B."

Sarah managed a feeble wave, but Gemma sprinted after them leaving her and Tyler alone. "I'll be right back," she trilled. "Don't do anything before I return." The girl sounded positively gleeful.

Clearly Gemma was having the time of her life, Sarah thought miserably. She forced a smile to her lips and spoke to Tyler. "I can't believe you're here. What made you take the trip? Especially...considering everything."

"I just decided, last minute, to come see the love of my life," he said. "Is there a problem?" A frown creased his forehead. "You don't look very happy to see me." He ran a hand through his sandy hair and glanced back to where Gemma stood talking to the others. "Just why were you alone with *that guy* anyway?" He sounded antagonistic. Sarah took a deep breath and tried to calm her nerves.

"I don't really think that's any of your business, but we all started out together this morning until Gemma hurt herself and didn't think she could walk. She and Gabrielle went back to Vernazza, so she could take it easy and not strain her knee—which actually seems much improved." Sarah just realised that Gemma hadn't been favoring the knee at all. In fact, her friend had just jogged across the pier and up the uneven cobblestones. Strange. "I'm surprised Gemma didn't explain all this."

He reached for his bag and shrugged it over one arm, looking at her angrily. "Not my business? I just flew halfway around the world to see you!"

"Anyway," she continued, trying to diffuse the situation until they were somewhere private. "I'm glad to see you, of course. It's just a bit of a shock since we broke up and you never like to travel or leave your work." Anxiety rose in her throat, threatening to close it off. She coughed. "I—I think we should follow them Tyler, it's getting too dark to see." Sarah gazed at the moon, suspended above them like an eerie globe. Had it been a good or a bad omen? Five minutes ago, she'd been deliriously happy. How quickly things could change.

The lights of the village offered a golden glow that extended into the water for some distance, but still, Sarah had no desire to stand here with Tyler so soon after she'd been with Raphaël.

Together they walked slowly to shore and up the embankment. Gemma hurried back to them; her face wreathed in smiles.

"Gabrielle says she'll meet us back in Vernazza for a drink if we want. Raphaël seems to think he might turn in for the night, but we'll see about that. What do *you* say?" She brushed past Sarah and took Tyler's arm. "That okay with you?"

"Well, I came here to see Sar..." he started saying, but Gemma cut him off.

"So! You'll still be with her. Anyway, I want to see you too." She laughed, but he didn't return her teasing.

"Do you mind? I'd like to talk to Sarah alone." Tyler's voice sounded firm.

Gemma dropped his arm. "You don't have to get all huffy about it. Fine. I'll ride back to Vernazza with Gabrielle and leave you by yourselves." In a loud stage whisper, that Sarah could tell was meant for Tyler to hear, she continued. "You and Raphaël looked pretty cozy out there under the moon." With that parting shot, Gemma stalked off, but at that moment Sarah heard the now familiar noise of the train as it left the station and picked up speed.

"Wait!" Sarah called urgently. Even though Gemma appeared to have gone all weird on her, the very last thing she wanted was to be alone with Tyler tonight. Tomorrow she'd have to tell him he'd come here for nothing, but tonight she couldn't face the scene. She couldn't wrap her head around the fact that he'd come here in the first place. "There won't be another train for fifteen minutes. Why don't we all go for a gelato and then we'll take the train together."

"Great." Gemma's good humour was restored. She began chattering about what she'd done to fill her day.

Tyler still looked upset, his eyes telling her they needed to talk. However, he followed reluctantly as she led them to a gelateria she'd spied on the street not far away. Sarah was surprised she could think at all after what had happened. First the kiss of a lifetime, then her ex-boyfriend shows up with Gemma who'd gone all, 'Single White Female' on her.

Gemma kept up a running commentary the whole way, making it unnecessary for anyone to speak at all. Within minutes, they were standing inside the diminutive shop and staring down at the many gleaming, metal tubs of Italian ice cream.

A round-faced man with thinning hair and a pristine apron bustled through a door from a back room ready to serve with his scoop. Tyler stared, a frown creasing his forehead at the board listing all the varieties above the man's head. Clearly, he wasn't happy to be here.

"No problema," the man repeated several times as Tyler hummed and hawed. "I give you samples, yes?" He filled tiny plastic spoons with the various flavours and handed them over the counter for Tyler to try.

After much deliberation, they ordered. Sarah paid for them all since she was the only one with cash, and they stepped onto the street again to savour the cool air of the evening and the delectable frozen treats.

"Delicious," declared Gemma. She swirled her dark chocolate and coffee mixture together, rolling her eyes as she spooned it into her mouth.

Tyler, who after lengthy consideration had asked for a serving of vanilla, ate his in silence, stealing the odd look at Sarah as they strolled back toward the train station.

She pointedly ignored his attention. Soon enough they would be compelled to talk it through. She mentally prepared herself, knowing he would not take what she had to say very well. She was done with him in every sense of the word, friend or otherwise. This latest move of his was stalker material. She still couldn't wrap her head around it. Tyler didn't do anything spontaneously. It was very out of character.

She took the first taste of pistachio gelato and allowed the creamy goodness to melt on her tongue. Even in the midst of a crisis it was impossible not to find it fabulous. She should have been eating gelato every day. Tomorrow she would order it morning, noon, and night. Then she remembered that tomorrow night she would be leaving not only the Cinque Terre, but Raphaël. What must he be thinking of her? To him it would look as though she'd had a boyfriend back home and was fooling around with him, here. *Ugh!*

With a sigh she led the way back to the long tunnel that connected Via Colombo to the train station. It was long and rather dark, but thanks to lights recessed into the side of the rock walls, they could see.

"Do you have a ticket?" she asked Tyler as they slowly shuffled along.

"I have a pass for two days. Will that work?"

"Of course," Gemma answered. "Come on. I think the train is coming now."

Finishing the last of the gelato on the train platform, they discarded the paper cups and spoons in a receptacle. Then stood together waiting while the train whistled in. It screeched to a halt. Gemma appeared oblivious to the strained silence that surrounded her. She followed Tyler onto the train, asking him about his flight, and threw herself down in the seat beside him. Sarah took the one opposite and stared sightlessly out the window.

What a terrible ending to a fantastic day. She should have explained about Tyler over dinner. But would it have helped? Maybe not. She would still have looked like a cheating girlfriend in Raphaël's eyes. The train rolled down the track, quickly picking up speed. She could see the lights from homes sprinkled on the hillsides above them as they burst out of one tunnel and flew into the next. And still the endless drone of Gemma's voice went on. Sarah caught Tyler's eyes. He rolled them ever so slightly and gave her a crooked smile.

She wasn't capable of smiling back. But then a horrible thought struck her and she broke rudely into Gemma's discourse to ask Tyler a question. "Where are you staying? It must be impossible to find a hotel or B&B at the last minute. I imagine they're all booked up."

What if he had intended on staying in her room? That was completely out of the question. Thank goodness she only had a single bed and very little space. He wouldn't even be able to sleep on the floor.

Gemma answered for him. "I asked Luna. They only have the four rooms to let, and, of course, they're full. She didn't think he'd feel comfortable in the public sitting room on a sofa, so she found him a collapsible cot and put it in a storage space."

Had Gemma *always* been this intrusive? First she babbled non-stop at the man, and now she wouldn't give him the opportunity to speak for himself. Sarah felt as though her eyes had been opened on a number of counts this night.

"Good." Sarah placed her hands on her knees and leaned forward to direct her question at Tyler only. He looked drained. "What time did your flight arrive? You've gotten here so late."

"Around noon." He reached out and placed a hand over one of hers and she fought the urge to flinch away. "It took me a while to figure out where you were, but Gemma helped. Then, we couldn't reach you." His eyes had a puzzled look in their depths. "I want to know why you were with that French guy when Gemma said—"

"Gemma knew you were coming?"

"She helped me with directions on how to get here," he said evasively, lifting his hand and sitting back. "It was meant to be a surprise. A good surprise," he added bitterly. "I still don't understand why you spent the day alone with Raffia, or whatever the hell his name is."

Sarah didn't know how to respond without lying. It hadn't been a good surprise. Not at all. She glanced at Gemma and caught the girl with an almost triumphant look on her face as she bent to retie a shoelace.

"We'll talk later," Sarah said. "I don't think a public train is the place for it. Do you?"

Tyler shook his head as though to reset his brain and rolled up the sleeves of his sweater. "I knew it would be hot, but this is crazy." He wiped perspiration from his brow and peered out the train window. "It's really bright outside."

"There's a full moon tonight," Gemma piped in. "Strange things can happen." Grinning, she wiggled her fingers in a way that suggested otherworldly sorts of things.

Out the windows, on the opposite side of the train, Sarah could see the silvery sheen of *la lune* riding the waves of the Ligurian Sea. Her thoughts slipped back to Raphaël. Unconsciously, she raised fingers to her mouth still feeling his kisses.

Their train drew to a halt in Manarola. People left. People bustled in. The train paused a few minutes and then was off again.

"You must be exhausted," Sarah said, noticing Tyler yawn.

"Yeah, it's been a long day." He stifled another yawn. "I've got to get to bed once we're back. I can't do any more." He slid down in his seat and leaned sideways, resting his head on the window.

"Don't fall asleep now!" Gemma warned, giving him a little shake. "It isn't far to Vernazza." She patted Tyler's arm solicitously, sliding her own around his back and trying to lean him toward herself. "We have to climb a short distance to the B&B too," she warned.

"To say we must 'climb a *short* distance' is debateable," Sarah said with a grimace. "At least you have a backpack though. The trek shouldn't be too bad."

"I'll carry it for you," Gemma broke in again.

She would? Sarah widened her eyes as she contemplated her friend. Gemma was going to some odd lengths to ensure Tyler's comfort. Certainly, more than she'd done for her.

"I don't need help." Tyler slumped against Gemma and she smiled proudly at Sarah over his head.

The group lapsed into silence. A few minutes later, they arrived.

Shouldering his bag, Tyler staggered down the train steps and slowly the trio made their way up to The Point. Sarah offered to carry his bag for him, as did Gemma—several times, but he insisted on lugging it himself, despite yawning every five steps or so.

Thanks to the aid of a small flashlight Gemma had purchased earlier with Gabrielle, they finally reached the floodlit doorway. Sarah fished out her set of keys, slid them into the lock, and pushed inside.

A dim light was on in the kitchen and they passed through quickly.

"Luna said she'd leave a note with instructions in here," Gemma whispered, as they turned the corner by the staircase. She and Sarah removed their own backpacks and set them on the bottom step before proceeding. With Gemma leading, they entered a warm sitting room they hadn't seen before.

There were no dark, wooden beams in this space. The walls were painted a creamy white and long beige bookcases stood on either side of a fireplace at one end of the room. It wasn't a wide area. Two tan-coloured sofas faced one another at the mid-point, while matching easy-chairs sat at both ends, sharing a long coffee table littered with brochures and books on discovering the Cinque Terre.

Two double doors with latticed glass, led to a deck outside that was flooded in moonlight, and next to that a television was bolted to the wall. Everywhere were plants. They trailed over the bookcases and sat in large clay pots on the floor. In the soft light from two large table lamps the overall effect was cozy and welcoming.

Gemma made straight for the note, pinned to one chair, and tore it off to scan the words.

"Luna prepared a bed for him through there," she said, looking up and pointing to the far end of the room where a narrow door, painted the same cream colour as the walls, was almost completely swallowed up by a nearby Boston fern.

Tyler shrugged off his backpack and let it hang from his hand. "Lead me to it. I'm wiped."

Gemma strode across the room and grasped the ancient-looking latch. "She's also left you towels and soap, but says you'll have to use one of our bathrooms for bathing as the only other one with a tub or shower is in their private living space."

Tyler nodded wearily. Sarah, bringing up the rear, brushed past the thick foliage, to gingerly navigate two steps down in the wavering beam of Gemma's flashlight. The young woman marched to where a long silver chain glinted at the center of the room. She grasped it and pulled.

The place flooded with bright light, causing Sarah to blink. She swivelled around to see they were completely surrounded by shelves. Rows upon rows of preserves and wines lined one wall, while cans, dry goods, extra towels, and bed linens filled the others. There was one tiny window in the far corner on the top left, but it was closed tight. On the polished wooden floor, pushed against stacks of cellophane wrapped toilet paper, tissues, and extra pillows, was a cot.

"This looks great." Tyler immediately flipped his bag onto the floor and kicked off his shoes. "I'll see you both tomorrow, okay?" He opened his arms to Sarah. After a long pause, she moved in to give him a quick hug, but kept him at a distance. "I'll come find you in the morning." he mumbled before dropping onto the little bed.

"G'night Gemma," he said with a wave. "Thanks for arranging this." He patted the blankets and smiled before toppling onto them with another drawn-out yawn.

"No problem," Gemma said in a rather deflated voice. She made for the doorway and disappeared.

At this point, all Sarah wanted was to run as far away from this place as possible, but she couldn't.

Reaching up, she snapped off the light. Then, she groped her way back to the steps and into the sitting room, pulling the door not quite closed so Tyler could see if needed. She scanned the room, thinking Gemma would be waiting for her. No. She wanted to have a word with the woman, to get a little clarity on the crazy situation that had taken place this evening. But her friend was nowhere to be seen. Sarah retrieved her bag, noting Gemma's was still there, and hurried upstairs.

Her sharp rap on Gemma's blue door availed nothing. She tried the handle. Locked. Sarah pondered this a moment, feeling as though her friend had been right. There was something quite otherworldly going on tonight.

With nothing else to do but turn in early herself, she found her keys and opened her own, yellow door.

Flinging her bag on a chair beside her, Sarah bent to

unfasten her sandals. It felt good to stretch her toes in the cool night air. She slumped onto the bed, rubbing life back into her feet, and gazed through the glass door. It was so bright outside. Rising, she walked over, pulled it open, and stood in the gap, enjoying the slight breeze that ruffled through the thin curtains. Then, she poked her head out, making sure no one was there before she stepped onto the terrace.

Tiptoeing to the railing, she leaned over it, her mind whirling. The emotions she'd felt for Raphaël this day had been overwhelming. She closed her eyes and relived a few, her heart swelling. They were more powerful and went deeper than anything she'd ever shared with Tyler. And, if he was honest with himself, she didn't believe Tyler felt anything earth-shattering for her either. They were friends and comfortable with one another. But enough was enough. She was done with their friendship, too. The sooner she explained that to him, the better.

A sigh escaped her lips as she thought again of Raphaël. It wasn't enough that she'd dumped him the first time. No. She'd been dragged into a scenario that had pushed him away for a second time. There would be no returning from that, she was sure of it. She had effectively lost the only man she'd ever really cared about, just when things appeared to be going right.

Sarah lifted her face to a gentle wind that slipped up the rock face from the Liguria Sea, so far below. Subconsciously, she memorized the beauty of the moon shining through the sweeping branches of the oak tree ahead of her. It was peaceful; a welcome respite after the long day she'd had.

Small pebbles crunching under footsteps alerted her

to the presence of someone walking up the path. Stealthily, she moved to the other side of the sundeck and peered into the semi-darkness. It was Gemma, she was sure of it. The shadowy figure reached the front landing and keys jangled together as the door was unlocked. Then, a soft click told Sarah her friend was inside. She doubted Gemma would come to her door and found she was glad for it. She had a lot of questions, but they could wait until tomorrow. Gemma was a bit of an enigma right now. Sarah didn't think she would get straight answers even if she asked questions directly.

Moving across the platform to her vantage point, Sarah caught the insistent beep of her cell phone. Flinging the curtain wide, she rushed into her room and snatched it off the bed.

"Hello," she said in a low voice.

"Hi sweetie." The soft, comforting voice of her cousin Angelina brought instant tears to Sarah's eyes. "Hope it's not too late? I just wondered how things were going?"

Blinking the moisture away, Sarah stiffened her back and drew a cleansing breath. "It's never too late to hear from you. And things are okay. It's so beautiful here I don't want to leave, to be honest." With the phone held to her ear, she wandered back to the door and closed it lest anyone overhear.

Angelina laughed. "I knew you'd feel like that. Does your friend Gemma like it too?"

"Yes." Since her efforts to talk to Gemma had been thwarted, Sarah decided to confide, at least partially, in her cousin. "Raphaël is here. Staying at the same B&B as we are. Can you believe it? How bizarre is that?"

Sarah sat on her bed and flopped backward, staring into the darkness.

"Oh no..." There was a pause at the other end, and then Angelina spoke. "You and Gemma are staying with Romeo and Luna? But why would she do that?"

"What do you mean?" Sarah frowned. It almost sounded as though Angelina knew something.

"I knew Raphaël was going to spend time with Gabrielle and his friends who own the B&B. But when your friend called me out of the blue to ask about the Cinque Terre, I had no idea she'd plan to take you to that exact location."

"Gemma called...You?" Sarah's hand clenched around her cell phone. She was thoroughly mixed up now.

"I admit, it did surprise me to hear from your school friend, considering I've never met her. She must have looked up the business number of the winery. I was given a message that she'd rung and was asking for my private phone number. Out of concern for you, I gave it. She called me a few weeks ago. Explained who she was and that she was worried for you. She thought you were pushing yourself too hard and needed a break from teaching before you went home."

"Unbelievable," Sarah murmured, feeling shock radiate through her. "Gemma knew exactly where to go to set me up with Raphaël and then pretend it was fate. But why set me up like that?" Sarah twirled a long tendril of hair around her finger, her mind racing as she remembered Tyler, in his sleepiness on the train, revealing that Gemma had known he was coming here. Heck! She had probably invited him. It was elaborate, for sure, but suddenly the pieces fell together in Sarah's mind.

"I don't know how she'd have known Raphaël would be there at this exact time though," Angelina said, her voice worried. "Unless I mentioned it and don't remember. I recall she asked where our family stayed if we visited the area. I must have told her. Oh Sarah, I'm so sorry."

"I think Gemma set us all up," Sarah said in a low, wondering tone. "My ex-boyfriend arrived here tonight. Can you believe that? She always hated the fact that I dated him. She tried everything she could to talk me out of doing it, but it was Tyler that pursued me. Not the other way around." She leapt from the bed and began to pace.

"She's gone to some extreme measures, if that's the case," said Angelina. "I'm concerned about you. The woman sounds unhinged."

"It's weird alright." Sarah recalled so many things that now made sense. Gemma had insisted they visit the Cinque Terre on these specific days and offered to set up all the arrangements. Her friend's constant reminders that fate must be bringing Sarah and Raphaël together for a greater purpose. Not to mention all the little tricks she'd pulled to give them time alone. Sarah wondered if Gemma had actually thrown herself off the ferry to create a scenario where she and Raphaël would be alone all day.

It was like living in a third-rate movie filled with lying, deception, and espionage. Had Gemma contrived this situation in the twisted belief she was helping Sarah to find happiness with a past love? It didn't make sense.

There had to be another reason. What was at the root of it all? Trying to figure it out threw Sarah's heart into turmoil.

"I remember now!" Angelina said hesitantly and with evident regret. "I hedged about giving her details, but she was insistent. She told me you wanted to see the town in the Cinque Terre that Raphaël had often spoke of and the B&B ran by his friends. Said she wanted to surprise you with a trip there."

"You didn't think that might be awkward?" Sarah felt her agitation building. She rose to her feet and paced back and forth across her room. "What if Raphaël was here? Which, of course he is."

"I thought she'd have enough sense not to do that," Angelina's voice trembled. "I'm so sorry Sarah sweetie. Are you okay?"

"Yeah, I'm just great." Sarah knew she sounded bitter, but couldn't help it. Her friend had deceived her on purpose, then pretended it had been destiny that brought her and Raphaël together. But why would Gemma care so much about her love life? She'd told the woman about Raphaël years ago. It wasn't like she brought him into every conversation.

"I had no idea you were headed to the coast. Much less to that particular B&B," Angelina continued sorrowfully. "Ugh…What have I done?" She groaned.

"You didn't do anything," Sarah assured her. "You're completely innocent in this. However, Gemma is going to have a lot of explaining to do. She set me up! Raphaël too! And I think perhaps Tyler as well." Sarah began winding a whole wad of her hair around her hand. Her pacing quickened. "He had thought I somehow contrived to be here with him! Argh!"

"So, has it been bad? Have you managed to avoid one another?" Angelina's voice was strained. "I can't help but blame myself."

Sarah held her forehead in a weary hand, striding back and forth. "It didn't begin well, but things got... better. Fabulous in fact. Until tonight when Tyler arrived on the scene."

"Tyler? Isn't he the man who's asked you to marry him ten times? *Mon Dieu!* This has gone from bad to worse. You think your friend had something to do with that too?"

Through the phone line, Sarah could hear Angelina had begun pacing too. Despite her agitation, Sarah felt like giggling hysterically. This whole trip had been like living in a poorly done soap opera.

"Yes," she sighed heavily. "Although ten is a bit of an exaggeration. It was only once, and I said no. But he's been more than persistent." Feeling her body go weak, she flopped back on the bed. There wasn't enough room to properly pace in here anyway.

"I can't help but think Gemma's at the bottom of that too. She's been determined to get Raphaël and I back together ever since we arrived."

"She has? Doesn't it seem odd that she'd ask your boyfriend to join you? Maybe you're mistaken."

"Maybe," Sarah agreed doubtfully. "But I don't think so. Something tells me she orchestrated that particular mess as well."

"Wow. And I thought you'd given up on drama." Angelina stifled a disbelieving giggle. "You seemed destined to marry the guy next door and live the uneventful life of an elementary school teacher. Clearly I had that all wrong."

"You and me both." Sarah sighed deeply. "But I don't want to monopolize the conversation with my troubles. How is everyone where you are? I'd love to come see Celeste and baby Philippe. He looks so much like Julien. The pictures you've sent were so sweet."

"We're fine. Celeste is a love, naturally. And Philippe is into everything now. I have to lock all the cupboard doors." Angelina laughed. Then her voice became anxious. "To be honest, I'm worried about this situation, and you. What are you going to do?"

"I don't know how it'll all play out. First thing tomorrow I'm going to talk with Gemma, and then I'm telling Tyler I want nothing more to do with him..."

"Wait a moment. Tyler came there to propose —again?"

"That's what Gemma said." Sarah thrust her legs in front of her, feet dangling over the side of the bed.

"And just how does she know this?" Angelina's concern deepened. "You have a problem with that so-called friend of yours," she declared.

"I know. Believe me, I'll deal with her in the morning." Sarah smoothed the bedspread beneath her restless hand. "Anyway, I'd better get to sleep. Talk to you soon, okay? Love you."

"Talk to me tomorrow, you mean! I want to know what happens. Love you too, Sarah. Take care of yourself."

They wished one another a good night and hung up. Sarah remained where she was. Sleep seemed very far away at the moment. Taking into account all that would happen tomorrow, this might be the last bit of peace she'd have until she was home again.

Feeling as though she'd aged about twenty years, Sarah hauled herself upright and turned off her phone, hoping she hadn't spoken loud enough to be heard next door.

She'd like to have an opportunity to explain this mess to Raphaël and tell him how much she cared for him, but wondered if she'd ever be given the chance. With the light still off, she changed into her nightgown and padded to the bathroom where she shut the door quietly. Leaning on it she contemplated what tomorrow held in store for her.

She hadn't said a word to Angelina about the part that upset her the most. Raphaël would never be a part of her life after this fiasco. She'd lost him for good this time.

CHAPTER 11

A banging noise broke in on Sarah's restless sleep. Rolling over, she opened her eyes a crack to see sunlight streaming through the window over her head. She was irritated with herself. This was her last day, and she didn't want to waste any of it, but she wasn't surprised it was so late. She'd tossed and turned in bed until at least 3 a.m., unable to shut off her brain.

"Just a minute," she called, flipping the duvet back and digging her toes into the delicate pattern of the rug at her feet. Reaching for a sweater, she pulled it over her shoulders and drew it together across her chest before opening the door.

"Mornin'. Told you I'd come see you first thing." Tyler stepped across the threshold without invitation and strolled inside, making a face. "What a place. Glad I slept in the storage room." His eyes disdainfully swept over the room before he sat down on the bed and grinned at her, patting a spot next to him.

He looked great considering he'd spent the night in

little more than a broom closet. The long pants and sweater had been traded for some khaki shorts with a red and blue striped t-shirt, and sandals had replaced the loafers. He'd obviously shaved too and showered by the look of his damp hair. But whose bathroom had he used? Certainly not hers.

She could feel the colour draining from her face. So, the questioning was to begin before she'd even brushed her teeth. Well, so be it. She should get this over with.

"Tyler, I'd like to say something before you begin…"

"This isn't the time for talking, sweetheart," he drawled, interrupting her. "I have something I'd like to say to you too, but not now." He leaned forward, snaking an arm around her waist to pull her into his arms.

Immediately, she pushed away. "I want to talk, not snuggle. Plus, I need to get showered and dressed."

"I haven't even gotten a kiss yet." He let her go with a scowl. "What's going on? Does it have something to do with Rapherty…or whatever you call him?"

"No, it doesn't. And I broke up with you before I left for Italy. Remember?" Sarah nearly yelled. "There will be no kisses. I don't even know why you're here!"

Tyler's face flushed angrily. Without a word he strode out of the room, slamming the door behind him.

Dragging a hand across her forehead, Sarah sank onto her bed. This was going to be one horrible day. And her last one in the Cinque Terre too. But it had to be faced and now was the time to do it. She hurried to the chest of drawers and yanked one open to remove underwear and a top she'd purchased in Pisa. She shook it out, admiring the pretty, powder blue ruffles creating cap sleeves, and the thick shirring across the bottom ending in bows on either side. It showed a little of her toned midriff. She planned to wear her soft, high-waisted jean shorts with it and white sneakers. Grabbing some tiny gold hearts for her ears and a matching necklace, she made for the bathroom.

It didn't take long for her to shower and get dressed. She decided to let her hair dry naturally and combed it out to lay in a mass of golden curls down her back as she applied a light touch of gold eyeshadow, some mascara, and a rosy shade of lipstick. She needed the confidence boost brought on from knowing she looked good.

Tyler's words had been a catalyst, galvanizing her into action. This situation must not be allowed to continue. Fifteen minutes later, Sarah had re-entered the bedroom fully prepared to have the big discussion once she found him.

Quickly, she tidied her room and took the time to pack. Who knew where the day would go from here? She might as well be ready for whatever transpired. There was very little chance it would end well. Tyler heard nothing of what she'd said before leaving on this trip, or he'd purposefully chose to ignore it. It was becoming more and more apparent her thoughts and feelings were secondary to his own as he behaved like she was an obstinate child who needed help knowing her own mind.

She surveyed the room one last time, committing it to memory. She'd had a lovely time here, before Tyler arrived on the scene.

Slinging the day bag around her neck, she crammed her hat on her head and dragged the heavy silver suitcase out the door. Lifting it into her arms she staggered down the stairs. At least the walk to Vernazza wouldn't be quite as arduous as the climb up.

The clatter of dishes and voices told her Tyler was at the breakfast table with Gemma and Gabrielle for sure, but she couldn't hear Raphaël. No shock there. She doubted whether she'd see him again in her lifetime, let alone for breakfast.

Yet, to her surprise, he *was* there, standing outside on the deck with his back to the open patio doors, a porcelain cup in his hand. Her heart thumped in her chest. With effort, she dragged her eyes away from his broad shoulders and back to the table. The other three were sitting together; the two women sitting opposite to Tyler laughing at a story he was telling.

"And that's when they yelled, 'Hey lady. Get off the sidewalk!'" Tyler guffawed loudly as he swivelled in his chair amid the general laughter of his punchline. "Sarah! You look beautiful," he said. "Come sit beside me and I'll get you a cappuccino."

"I'd rather chat," she said, meeting his eyes squarely. "Could we go for a walk?"

"Okay, but Luna's gone to all the trouble of making extra food for us. It's rude to just leave." With a sweeping arm he gestured toward the sideboard and its wide array of delicacies. At the same moment, Luna herself rounded the corner bearing a tray with two more coffees. One was for Sarah.

"*Grazie*," Sarah nodded her gratitude to the smiling woman. "It smells wonderful."

Accepting the hot cup, she dropped with resignation into the chair Tyler had pulled out for her. Her gaze strayed to Raphaël, but he had moved away from the window and beyond her view.

Tyler turned on the charm for the ladies and launched into another hilarious tale. Sarah had heard them all before. Sipping at her steaming drink, she watched Gemma and Gabrielle's reactions. The latter listened to him with a half-smile curving her luscious lips, her eyes glittering with mirth and her long dark hair perfectly accented by the short, ruby-red dress she wore. Gemma, on the other hand, wore her usual garb— a pair of sensible, khaki cargo shorts and a plain white t-shirt. Though she'd taken care to apply a pale pink lipstick and some frosted eyeshadow. Her hair was curled instead of pulled back into the customary pony-tail. That was different.

Sarah allowed Tyler's voice to wash over her without listening. She considered the sight before her. Gemma had known Tyler the longest of any of them, but she leaned on one hand, smiling across the table at the man as though he'd just dropped from Heaven; the best thing since 3D movies.

"Tyler, you're so funny," Gabrielle snorted into her coffee, threatening to spill it as she laughed at some-thing he'd said.

The casual remark had an effect on Gemma. Her face flushed red as a beet, and she gripped the cup in her hand until her knuckles turned white. Sarah could have sworn she heard the woman's teeth grind together.

Straightening, Sarah took a gulp of her drink. How could she have been so blind all this time? It was as though someone had flipped the light switch in her brain and she saw everything clearly now. Gemma was in love with Tyler and had been for years.

She recalled other instances in her relationship with Tyler when Gemma had begged to come along and then tried to monopolize his attention. Sarah had watched it happen almost indulgently, believing her friend was simply missing the company of a man.

Yet clearly Sarah had refused to see the situation for what it was. Betrayal. There had even been a few circumstances when Sarah couldn't go with Tyler to an event—so Gemma went in her place. It hadn't bothered Sarah at the time. Though looking back, she wondered if it was because she hadn't really loved him anyway.

It felt as if she was looking at her friend for the very first time and she didn't like what she saw. Gemma had manipulated her and convinced her to come to the Cinque Terre under the guise of needing a holiday. Only she had purposely thrown Sarah together with Raphaël. Not for Sarah's benefit. Oh no. For Gemma.

If she could get Sarah out of the way, the playing field would be clear for her to snap up the man she wanted to have for herself—Tyler. As a last resort, Gemma must have begged him to come here, hoping he'd see Sarah and Raphaël together and break things off himself.

Now Gemma's eyes were throwing knives at Gabrielle. Sarah suddenly realised that Gemma considered every woman who even looked at Tyler to be a rival. But it was to no avail since Tyler didn't love anyone but himself. Sarah flinched as Tyler slid an arm around her shoulders. He didn't love her, and he probably didn't love Gemma either. He was only out for himself, and the wealth Sarah represented. Take over her father's company indeed! She saw it all clearly now.

Throughout her life she'd dealt with people wanting to get close to her solely because of her parents' money. Because Gemma and Tyler were her friends, she'd trusted them to her own detriment. It was awful to think her closest friends were so duplicitous.

A vision flitted through her mind. What would happen if Raphaël asked her to marry him? With a twisting stab to her heart, she knew her answer would be very different. But that relationship was over. It wouldn't help her cope with the present circumstances by torturing herself.

Wow. Three revelations in one morning. Sarah pushed back her chair and stood, causing Tyler's arm to fall away. The Cinque Terre was turning her into a new woman.

"I'm going for a walk," she announced. Looking meaningfully at Tyler, she reached for her hat and rammed it onto her head. "Alone." Snatching her bag and glasses off the table where she'd set them, she marched from the room. She didn't need any of these people—Raphaël included.

"Wait!" Tyler yelled, scrambling up to follow her, but she quickened her step and slammed the front door in his face.

The Azure Trail beckoned to her. She needed to clear her thoughts before making the journey back to La Spezia tonight, or maybe she'd leave right now. After all, what would she do with these people all day after she delivered the unpleasant news to Tyler? Thank goodness she'd be alone for the flight back to Canada. It crossed her mind that Gemma must have changed her original travel plans, because she hoped she would be staying behind with Tyler. They should be together, she thought. They deserved one another.

Through the wooden gate she went, her bag flung over her shoulder and dark sunglasses saving her eyes from the glare of the rising sun. She looked back. Good. No one appeared to be following her, so she struck out away from Vernazza, toward Corniglia.

She hadn't gone more than a few steps when she heard pounding footsteps. Moments later, a breathless Tyler appeared at her side, catching her hand and bringing it to his lips.

"Sweetheart," he exclaimed, "is something wrong? Why did you take off on us?"

She stopped and rounded on him. "Go back Tyler. I'd like to be alone." He stood in shocked silence, his mouth working, but no words coming out. Clearly this was not how he expected the visit to have gone.

"What's gotten into you anyway?" His mouth tightened. "You must know I came here to be with you."

"After what we talked about before I left the country two months ago, I honestly don't understand why you would come here—" Sarah changed her mind with decisiveness. "But you're right. We should talk now." Spying an outcropping of rock higher up the mountain and away from the public path, she pointed. "Let's sit up there."

Without waiting for his agreement, she began to climb. Pulling herself up the steep slope by grabbing branches and hauling herself over rocks and debris, she reached the gigantic rock and heaved herself onto it. It was secure, but its base tilted toward the hillside and the sea. Under other conditions she would have loved to sit here with a good book and enjoy the view. She lifted her face to the warm Italian sun as she waited for Tyler to catch up. Sarah's thoughts felt clearer than they had in years. He scrambled up beside her, a dark look on his face and began to speak.

"I'd like to know what the he—" Smoothly she cut in.

"Shhh," she shushed him as one would an errant child. "I'm not answering your questions today Tyler. I'm speaking first. I'm truly sorry you came all this way. I imagine Gemma told you it would be a good idea, didn't she?" He nodded, albeit reluctantly.

"Thought so." She took a deep breath and stared toward the deep blue of the sea. "I need to reiterate something you chose to ignore." She shuffled around to look him straight in the eye. "I won't marry you, ever. It's not that I don't care about you, I actually hope you'll be very happy and have a great life. It's just, I don't love you and at this moment I don't even like you." She searched his face. "Apart from our other differences, we never had any..." she grasped for the right word. "Any spark."

"Spark?" Tyler appeared at a loss for words. "Are you kidding me? What do you mean, spark? Are you talking about chemistry? You never let me get close enough to find out!" Dropping his head, he rubbed a hand across the back of his neck. "Do you realise I just flew halfway around the world to propose?" He turned to glare at her. "And for what? To find out you're breaking up with me. How do I explain that to people? I'll look like a fool."

"I told you two months ago Tyler...you just didn't listen. I suggest you tell anyone who decided it's their business to know, that you and I finally realised we weren't right for one another. That we parted amicably knowing it was the right thing to do."

"But I *don't* think it's the right thing to do. I think we're invested in this relationship and we're good together." He picked up a pebble and hurled it into the brush. "Why are you doing this? Is it because of that guy you were with?"

"No."

"It is, isn't it?" Tyler's voice rose in anger. "You just don't want to admit it, because that might make you look like a cheater. It might tarnish your perfect image. I'm right, aren't I?"

"Tyler, the truth is I don't love you and I honestly believe you don't love me either." She held up a restraining hand as he leaned forward to protest crowding her. "I think we were friends, but we don't have what it takes to build a life together."

Then another voice chimed in as the scrabble of boots told them someone else was joining them on the rock. Sarah had been so intent on making Tyler see reason, she'd failed to notice the arrival of an outsider.

"You're both right." Gemma's head appeared over the boulder, and in a moment she bounded up beside them. "But I do."

Tyler looked dazed. "You do what?" he said, shaking his head and looking back and forth between the two women. "Why are you always showing up?" He leveled an angry glare at Gemma.

"I *do* love you." Ignoring Sarah, Gemma shuffled

around until she was on her knees directly in front of him. She moved close enough to lay her hands on his legs. "I've always loved you. Ever since my big breakup... you remember when you were so consoling and kind? I knew then that there was no one else in the world for me, only you."

"Umm, this is kind of a lot to take in right now Gemma...I was talking with Sarah. So, if you'll excuse us we—" Tyler only got a few words out before Gemma interrupted again.

"She doesn't love you. I do. Just forget her," Gemma said brusquely. "She loves Raphaël. If you had any sense, you'd see it." Then her voice softened. "Do you remember that first night?" She leaned over him, her eyes pleading that he recall the moment her feelings had changed. She grasped his hands.

The anger on Tyler's face turned to the look of fear on a cornered animal. Stunned, he glanced from side to side as though searching for an avenue of escape. "Look Gemma, you need to get a grip on yourself and leave us alone. Go back to the B&B. You've caused enough trouble. Why did you tell me I should come here?"

"Trouble?" she shrieked. "You idiot. I've waited for you ever since that night, five months, two weeks and four days ago, loving you from the sidelines when you offered her the only thing I ever wanted. And you tell *me* I'm trouble!" Tears rolled unchecked down Gemma's face. She sat back on her heels to wipe them away. Then she turned her anger on Sarah who'd been quite happy to stay out of this messy scene.

"It's your fault. You never loved him. I told you not to even start. I hate you!" Gemma crawled closer to

Sarah who cautiously edged away. Honestly, with her quick change of character and elaborate manipulations the girl was deranged.

"We slept together that night." An evil smile twisted Gemma's features. "In fact, we got together whenever you weren't around too."

Sarah reeled back. What? This revelation was completely unexpected. She didn't think her best friend and the man who'd professed his undying love for her could do such a thing. She shook her head to clear the fog.

"Hurts doesn't it?" Gemma continued, grinning like the Cheshire cat. "Maybe you're not as important as you thought you were...or maybe you're only desirable because of your family's money?"

Sarah's brain was spinning. Could it be true? One look at Tyler's furious face and Gemma's spiteful one told her everything. This was far worse than she'd imagined. Feeling a need to put as much distance between herself and them as possible, she shuffled away, peering over the edge of the rock to see if there was a way to climb down the other side. She needed to escape this madness.

"Sarah, you can't believe her." Tyler was pleading with her now. He reached out, grasping her wrist. Sarah yanked it away, feeling revulsion rise in her throat as he continued. "She's making it up. I've never been unfaithful to you, not with her or anyone. I love you."

Sarah felt as though she were dreaming. Reality blurred. Could this really be happening? She gripped the rock beneath her hands, running her fingers over the rough stone, trying to hold on to what was solid and dependable when the world around her was crumbling. Could her two closest friends have had an on-going affair right under her nose? It was inconceivable. Yet, even as her thoughts raced to deny it, her heart told her it was true. Why else would Gemma be so jealous? Why else would she have concocted this elaborate scheme, hoping Sarah would fall back in love with Raphaël and disappear. Gemma had never been her friend.

Memories flashed through Sarah's mind like bullets to her heart. Like the time she'd visited her parents and came back to campus early, only to find Tyler in the dorm room she shared with Gemma. They'd both looked dishevelled, but told her they were only studying together—and she'd been naïve enough to believe them.

Or the evening they'd all gone to a concert and Tyler had driven Gemma home, because the girl had complained of a headache. He'd insisted he do it alone so that Sarah could enjoy the rest of the show. But he'd been gone an hour and a half. The dorm was five minutes from the venue if that.

How could she have been so obtuse? In a stupor, she shuffled closer to the edge of the rock. The only thought in her mind was to get as far away from the pair of them as possible. But Tyler's fingers grasped her wrist again.

"Please, please don't do this. Think of the embarrassment we'll face," he said, tightening his grip and struggling to reel her back in. "Think of our parents, our friends. We can talk about it and work everything out. You'll see." He gave her a plastic smile that didn't reach his eyes.

"Stay away from me," Sarah said, her voice trembling. She shuffled as close to the edge of the rock as possible, struggling to escape. If only she could just disappear from this spot.

"Leave him alone!" Gemma screeched. "Don't touch her." The woman lunged at Sarah, springing from where she'd been rocking back and forth on her knees, her arms outstretched in an effort to knock Tyler's hand away.

In the process, she threw herself off balance. Losing traction on the slippery rock despite her hiking boots, Gemma slid backward at an alarming rate. She scrabbled for a foothold, scratching desperately with her fingers to hang on. Her eyes widened and she screamed as she toppled off the rock backwards.

Tyler lunged after Gemma, flinging himself across the face of the rock as he swiped the air, trying vainly to snag any part of her he could. But it was too late. With a dull thud, Gemma hit the ground below. It all had happened so fast, Sarah was dumbfounded. After Tyler scrambled off the rock, she shook herself from her paralysis to follow him.

Gemma lay on her side in a crumpled heap, moaning. Tyler flung himself into the scrub brush beside her with an exclamation of horror. Sarah dropped beside him and looked up at the boulder. Gemma had plummeted at least three metres. She sighed and turned back to assess the woman's injuries. Tyler was working to lift her, despite the steep incline, and was about to gather her into his arms.

"Stop!" Sarah grabbed his hands and held them still. "She shouldn't be moved...not until you know if her neck or spine were injured."

He nodded and bent over Gemma, placing his face close to hers. "Can you hear me, honey?"

Her eyes fluttered and she opened them just a crack, her tongue flicking across her lips before she tried to speak. "It's...my—my arm." Her brow furrowed with pain as she rolled onto her back and tried to push herself upright. "And maybe the right knee."

"She must not have hurt her spine, or her neck," Tyler said, his voice cracking with concern. He flashed a look at Sarah. "But she needs to see a doctor. How do we achieve that on this God-forsaken hillside? Is there one in Vernazza?"

As he spoke Gemma managed to sit up. Her face and arms were scratched from tumbling in the patch of dry shrubs, and her arm hung uselessly at her side, but apart from looking groggy, she appeared okay.

"The rumors of my death have been greatly exaggerated," she mumbled, famously quoting Mark Twain. Attempting a smile, she extended a hand to Tyler. "I want to stand, please, honey?" She looked at him with heavy lidded eyes, repeating the endearment he had used for her.

"Do you think that's wise?' He looked from her to Sarah and back again. "Did you hit your head?"

Gemma cautiously felt her scalp. "No bumps. It's good." She lifted her hand to him again, but her movements were slow and her speech drawling. "Please?"

He put an arm around Gemma and helped her to stand, favouring her leg. Sarah ripped the bag off her back and tore open the compartment where she kept her phone. She didn't have the number for their B&B, but she had the internet. This was not the first time she was grateful for the data package she'd paid for when arriving in Italy. Quickly, she found the phone number for The Point, hit the Call button, and waited anxiously for someone to pick up.

"*Ciao,* 'allo."

"Romeo! It's Sarah. We're on the hillside just below your house, heading toward Corniglia, but high up and off the path, not below. Gemma fell and we need help to get her to a doctor. Can you come?"

"*Bien sûr. Tout de suite.*" The call ended and Sarah shoved the phone into her shorts' pocket.

"Help's on the way," she told them. Gemma was examining her arm, biting her lower lip, and looking very pale. Tyler held tight to her, murmuring reassurances. Sarah stood there wringing her hands, not knowing what to say. They hadn't exactly been having a heart-warming chat when Gemma fell.

"Sarah," Gemma said, her voice edged in pain as she leaned heavily on Tyler's shoulder. "Maybe I shouldn't have brought that last part up...about Tyler and me hooking up—"

"Maybe...?" Sarah broke in, her voice raising with disbelief. She closed her eyes and willed herself to remain calm. "We can sort all that out later. First we need to get you to a doctor." She didn't want to hear anything further Gemma might want to say. She was done with the pair of them.

"I think you should both sit down until Romeo and Raphaël arrive," she continued. "There's no point in struggling to remain standing."

Gently, Tyler lowered the injured woman to the rocky hillside. Her head hung between her knees. Tyler dropped to sit beside Gemma, sliding an arm around her waist. It was all extremely awkward. Sarah stood in silence, forcing herself to stay calm and not just leave the pair of them to rot. With a bang, Sarah heard the gate shut and saw Romeo, Raphaël, and Gabrielle appear around a bend on the trail. Between them, the men carried an orange stretcher supported with two aluminium poles.

Sarah's eyes locked on Raphaël's the moment he spotted them. Grimly, he held her gaze as he climbed. Her heart felt as though it was being squeezed by an unseen hand and her mouth went dry. If only things could have been different. He acknowledged her with a nod, then looked away, his gaze softening as he pulled alongside of Gemma and took charge.

"Did you check for broken bones or concussion?" Raphaël turned his unsmiling regard on Tyler.

"Well, no, but...I mean, she was standing before you got here, so I think she's probably okay." He stepped back, openly flustered.

"That is not always proof. She could 'ave a fracture or a concussion and not be aware of it." Raphaël pulled a small flashlight from his back pocket. Bending, he smiled encouragingly to Gemma and explained what he was about to do. "I'm going to shine this light in your eyes to check for signs of concussion. Then, if you would lie on the stretcher, we will make sure you get to the doctor. There is an office in Monterosso al Mare and, of course, there is a hospital in La Spezia. You may decide where you would like to go. Do you understand?"

"Yes," she mumbled thickly, her body sagging with

pain. Flicking the light on, Raphaël beamed it from the outer corner of each eye inward.

"This is good," he said presently. "Your eyes respond quickly. I do not think you are in any danger. Now..." he motioned that Romeo should prepare the stretcher. "Let us 'elp you to lie down and stabilise your arm."

Romeo held the canvas stretcher steady as Raphaël and Tyler lifted the injured woman. Gabrielle gently laid Gemma's arm across her chest and supported it by securing a length of cloth looped around her neck so the jostling would not cause the arm to fall. Gemma was eased onto the makeshift bed without difficulty, and she relaxed with a groan. From a bag wound through his belt, Romeo produced several coiled straps. Handing two of the four to Raphaël, they knelt to secure their patient to the cot.

Gabrielle moved to slip an arm around Sarah's shoulders, and they stood together watching. "Are you okay?" she murmured. Sarah could only nod, but she appreciated the young woman's concern.

"I 'ave a car, but..." Romeo shrugged expressively, "it is up there." He jerked a thumb up the mountain they stood on. "We will get 'er onto a train. It is the simplest way, *d'accord?*"

"I want to go to the city," Gemma murmured.

Agreement was voiced and the group slowly moved down the hillside. Tyler and Romeo at the front and Raphaël at the back.

"I am fine," he said, waving away Sarah and Gabrielle's offer to assist him. "I 'ave the light end. But *merci.*" He gave them the briefest of smiles. Sarah fell

MOONLIGHT OVER THE CINQUE TERRE

back beside Gabrielle who linked arms with her and squeezed, offering silent reassurance.

As they made their way along the Azure Trail, Sarah thought of Gemma's bag with her identification and health insurance. It was still at the breakfast table, left behind in her hasty exit to follow them, but it would be needed. When the slow procession passed the gate to the B&B, she explained her mission in an undertone to Gabrielle, dashed through it and sprinted up the hill. When she reached the house, Luna was standing on the landing twisting a dish towel in her hands.

"I have been worried enough to make myself sick. Is she alright?" The lady hurried ahead of Sarah and threw open the front door for her to enter.

"I think she has a broken arm. She'll need to have it looked at by a doctor and be checked over to make sure though." Sarah hurried through the kitchen with the lady behind her. "I'm looking for her bag. She'll need her I.D. and health insurance," she called over her shoulder. Snatching it from the back of Gemma's chair, she spied her own silver case.

Should she take it? It would be awkward and in the way, but did she really want to return to this place of turmoil, only to collect a suitcase? The thought of spending any more time with Gemma, Tyler, or even the disapproving Raphaël was too much. Gemma and Tyler's revelations were something she needed to digest alone. Looking at the annoying, heavy case, she decided to take the dreaded thing along.

Snatching it from where she'd parked it against the wall, Sarah dragged the suitcase from the room.

"You are leaving? Now?" Luna looked puzzled.

183

"Please, do not feel you must. With all of these things happening I do not want that you should feel pressure. Go with your friends and leave your luggage here. Our next guests will not arrive until much later."

"It's best that I leave," Sarah said. Impulsively she hugged the little lady and kissed her cheeks. "It's almost checkout time anyway and I must go back to my room in La Spezia to pack tonight. If that's where we're taking Gemma I might as well go now, too."

"Ahh, I see. I hope you will return to stay with us again someday," Luna relented, a smile creasing her pretty face "And I pray that your friend Gemma will be okay." She shook her head. "Sometimes there are accidents on the trails of the Cinque Terre, but it is seldom they are life-threatening."

"I'm sure she'll be fine." Sarah dug into her shoulder bag for the keys to her room and pressed them into Luna's hand. "Thank you for the lovely stay. I really enjoyed myself here."

"You are most welcome," she said warmly. "Please, call me if there is anything I can do to help Gemma. She is booked to stay another two nights."

Interesting, Sarah thought ruefully, but she smiled as though she'd known this information all along. "I'll tell her to call you if she needs anything, Luna, but I'm pretty sure Tyler will be with her." Sarah rolled her case across the front landing. Taking the two steps down to the path, she waved and reached back to heft her heavy bag into her arms. "Bye," she called. Then, she dropped it onto its wheels and hurried down the path to the main trail.

Over parts of the Azure Trail, where the going

wasn't so rough, she dragged her case behind her not caring if it got damaged. However, for most of her harried flight down the hillside, Sarah carried the thing and was heartily sick of it before long. She tripped and stumbled over roots and rocks, over the roughly hewn stone steps until she vowed she'd garbage the heavy case before she ever took it on an excursion again. It was too much trouble.

The group with Gemma was faster than she'd expected, and she was much slower. They had nearly reached the village before she caught them again. She dropped her bag to the ground and fell into step behind Raphaël, feeling hot and sticky while puffing with exertion. Gabrielle was nowhere to be seen.

Lying still on the stretcher, Gemma was silent. Although she cradled her arm and moaned whenever she was jostled. High above the sun had really come into its own, baking the land and their little caravan.

Sarah took note of where Gemma had placed her good arm; bent across her face to ward off the scorching rays. She stepped up her pace to draw alongside them where the path had widened.

"Would you like my hat for shade?" she asked.

But Gemma mouthed the words, *no thanks*, not bothering to look at her.

Sarah shrugged, falling back behind again. She avoided catching Raphaël's eyes. What a wild holiday. Now after all Gemma had told her about the double life she and Tyler had led, she would nevertheless be guiding the two of them to the hospital. Good times.

Thankfully, she had a good idea where it was from having lived in the city for the summer. Then with any luck, she'd send the two of them back to the Cinque Terre and she'd head back to her rooming house near the school to collect the rest of her things.

She thought of the fear she'd seen on Tyler's face when Gemma fell, and the endearment he'd used when he bent over her crumpled body. He'd called her—honey. Sarah lifted a hand to remove her hat and wipe her brow. Not once, during the time they'd dated had he ever used that term with her. Maybe he really did have feelings for the woman?

Either way, Sarah didn't care. Her heart had been captured by another, five years ago in Provence. She felt unwanted moisture brim in her eyes and blinked furiously. This wasn't the time for tears and regret.

As if on cue, Raphaël turned his head to speak to her. "You went back for Gemma's passport and medical insurance?"

"Yes."

"Good girl. She is lucky to 'ave a friend such as you. And Tyler is..." His voice trailed off to nothing. They'd come to the last part of the path. It was paved and the going became easier, but still she could tell that the men were tiring. It couldn't be easy to lug someone down a rough trail in the boiling sun without fatigue.

Sarah wondered what Raphaël had been about to say. Did he also think Tyler lucky considering he was supposedly marrying her? Since last night's fiasco, Raphaël must believe she and Tyler were a couple, meaning she'd been cheating when she kissed Raphaël. What a tangled mess.

Was there any point in trying to disabuse him of the notion? Probably not—after callously dumping Raphaël five years ago, then conveniently showing up at his friends B&B and kissing him like she was trying to make up for lost time before her boyfriend arrived. She thought he must have been about to say something different, maybe like, *Tyler is going to need a lot of luck and patience if he's going to be with you.*

The men navigated the short flight of stairs down to the main street in Vernazza. Their patient lay still and pale, but uttered no complaint on the canvas bed.

It wasn't much further to the train station, which was good. Romeo, red-faced and panting, stopped before they ascended the two flights of steps to the overhead station platform. He turned to Raphaël and said a few words in French.

Raphaël chuckled, then translated. "Romeo says 'e is not in the shape 'e once was."

Tyler swivelled his head too. He stared at Gemma with concern, but said nothing. He continued to ignore Sarah. Focusing their attention on the last leg of the journey, the men took the stairs slowly. Raphaël lifted his end high over his head to compensate for the elevation of the steep staircase, then moved sideways as they navigated the bend and continued to the top.

Sarah, who had been dragging her case behind her, now stooped to lift it again. One last, horrible time. Laboriously, she took each step and then dropped the case to the pavement at the top with a bang.

People stood at the top waiting for the train. They stared with curiosity at Gemma on the stretcher. Raphaël glanced up at the digital screen for train times. "It is fortunate the train will be arriving in four minutes.

We will get you safely on board and then we will leave you in the capable hands of your friends."

"I want to walk now," Gemma said in a wavering voice that grew stronger as she continued. "It's just my arm. My knee hurts, but I've felt my leg and I don't think it's broken. There's no way I'm going to be carried into that train on a bed and laid in the aisle. Not gonna happen boys."

"Atta girl!" Tyler turned again with a broad grin and addressed the other two men. "Let's set her down over there." He indicated a quiet corner with a nod of his head. They moved to it, setting the stretcher down carefully, and bending over Gemma to help her rise. Tentatively, she got to her feet, supporting her arm with her good hand, and wincing with pain.

"Thanks for everything," she said, leaning on Tyler and balancing on one foot. "You guys were great. I've never been carried off the playing field before." Her attempt to make light of the situation fell flat. Romeo looked at her quizzically and Tyler jumped in to explain.

"Gemma's an athlete. You name a sport and she probably excels at it," he said proudly. "She just means she's never been carried away from a game, injured on a stretcher."

"Ah," said Romeo, inclining his head. "*Je comprends*, I understand. Do you 'ave tickets for this journey?"

Almost as though she had known when to appear, Gabrielle untangled herself from the crowd waiting for the train, and rushed to them, waving a ticket in her hand.

Romeo dipped his head in approval. "And Gemma? Where is 'ers?"

Gemma's face blanched even whiter. "I left everything at the house," she moaned.

"I have your bag." Sarah stepped forward and held it up.

"*Bien.*" Both Romeo and Raphaël answered in unison. Except Raphaël's gaze lingered on Sarah's face, his brow furrowing before he looked away. Her chest tightened and she fought to keep tears at bay once more.

"Then we will leave, if you will be alright getting onto the train?" Raphaël said politely.

"Yes," Gemma turned a thankful face to them. "You were wonderful. Thank you so much. We'll be back later, but I'll walk myself up the hill then." She smiled.

With a slight bow, Raphaël turned, marched across the platform, and disappeared into the stairwell leading back to the street.

"I won't be returning," Sarah said with a regretful look at Romeo who had paused a moment longer. "I want to thank you for your hospitality and the opportunity to stay in your lovely home."

"What!" he said in mock outrage, flinging his hands in the air. His gaze dropped to her silver bag. "And you carried that abominable case all the way down. You were supposed to allow me to 'elp you with it."

Sarah managed a half-hearted laugh. "It was fine. Coming down was much easier than climbing up. *Au revoir, et merci pour tout.*"

"Your French is *tres bien,* Sarah. I wish you a good journey, and you..." he gestured at the other two, and said, "Please 'ave a safe trip to see the doctor." With that, the man hurried away to catch his friend whose dark head could already be seen ascending the Azure Trail up the mountain.

Sarah looked longingly after him. Raphaël hadn't even said goodbye. Did he realise she was leaving? Perhaps not, he had been so intent on safely conveying Gemma to the train. He might not have even noticed she was dragging her case. Or perhaps he wanted to end things this way. A sob rose in her throat and she turned away to hide it, stemming tears with her fingers and wiping them away.

"Well, that's that," Tyler said. "The train should be here any second."

"Can I find your ticket for you, Gemma?" Sarah asked holding up the bag.

"Thanks, but Tyler will help me," Gemma said, not meeting Sarah's eyes. "In fact, you don't have to come at all. I think that might be best." She rested one leg against the wall behind her and turned her head stiffly to watch for the train with Tyler.

"Great." Sarah thrusted the bag into Tyler's hands and left them standing together. How quickly life could change. Dragging her case behind her, she crossed the platform and leaned on the barrier to take one last look at Vernazza. Beneath her hands the railing was smooth and warm from the heat of the early-morning sun. Via Roma, lined with tall, pastel-coloured houses curved away from her. The picturesque scene would remain in her memory like the muted frescoes she'd seen in museums of long forgotten cities.

The lane was alive with visitors and vendors all coming and going from shops, restaurants, and hotels. Balconies jutted from each building along the street, each one a dramatic stage with drying clothes as their backdrop and real people enacting Shakespeare's plays. She sighed as couples strolled by, talking, and laughing, some with their children. It was lovely, but the view was too heart-wrenching to linger.

She dreamt of strolling with Raphaël down this very street. Could it have been only yesterday that she had done that very thing? She could imagine his strong arms around her waist and the thrill of his breath on her cheek as he nuzzled her ear, whispering soft words of love. She knew now it was all she wanted, yet it was utterly unattainable.

Behind her the train flew into the station and squealed to a halt. Casting her dreams aside, she hustled back to the people she'd counted on as friends for what seemed so long, concerned Gemma might need help to board the train.

"Can I help?"

"No. We won't be needing you," Gemma said dismissing her. She looked at Sarah with a triumphant little smile and accepted Tyler's arm to help her climb the steps.

Sarah recoiled at the dislike and cruelty shining in Gemma's eyes. She stood rooted to the spot feeling as though her heart had been wrung out and hung on a line to dry. She was empty. She'd lost the only man she'd ever cared about and her two closest friends, all in one fell swoop.

"You getting on board, deary?" said a voice behind her. Sarah swivelled around to see an elderly white-haired couple beaming at her. The lady continued, "I take a little extra time to get on the train. If we don't hurry we're all going to miss it."

"Oh, sorry." Sarah blinked, feeling foolish. She grasped the rail and hoisted herself aboard, banging her suitcase up every step.

Taking note where Gemma and Tyler were sitting, she headed in the opposite direction, hoping there would be a spot that wasn't jammed with passengers. She was lucky. There was an open seat right on the aisle. She couldn't boost her suitcase onto the racks overhead. Instead, she pulled it as close to her legs as possible and rummaged for a tissue in the bag slung about her shoulders.

"Please take them," the little lady who'd spoken to her outside said, holding out a packet of tissues. "Are you okay?"

Sarah nodded mutely, not trusting herself to speak. She accepted the package with a wobbly smile and then turned away.

The tears would not obey her command to stop this time. They flowed down her face before she could blink them away. Yet she found a certain comfort in their salty taste. In a way, the last five years of holding back her emotions and putting on a mask of false contentment released from her.

Her thoughts were flooded with snippets of everything she had experienced at this wonderful destination, and the man with whom she had shared so much. All of it a dizzying array of moments that to her were the stuff of fairy tales. But there were too many words left unspoken, so many feelings not shared. And now it was too late. There was no happily ever after in this story, not for her.

She wiped her eyes, a gesture that seemed futile in the mass of overwhelming emotions she had experienced this morning. Sarah stared blearily out the window as the train rolled from the station. Her wayward tears creating a grey blur of movement in the reflected arms of waving bystanders, and streaking signs of the station as they gathered speed. The other passengers in the railcar were anonymous, chattering blobs in hats, beachwear, and sunglasses. They talked and laughed around her, the cacophony blending with the clanking and squealing of the train's wheels on the tracks below. Her senses melting into a sea of pain without the man she loved.

She closed her eyes, lifting a hand to soothe her furrowed brow, and lost herself in a memory. Raphaël's arms were once again around her waist, pressing her against the hard contours of his chest. She recalled the warmth of his skin, the faint scent of the sandalwood cologne he wore, and the sweet taste of his lips. And she remembered the silvery moon bathing them in its glowing benediction.

Just thinking of it caused her heart to pound and her breathing to quicken. Raphaël had evoked a response in her she hadn't known was possible. She desired to touch his face and trace the hard angles of his jaw and mouth. She took a deep, shuddering breath. It wasn't wise to dwell on this anymore. Sarah was leaving Raphaël behind in the gorgeous Cinque Terre and would never see him again. It was a closed door and she needed to focus on the future.

The last wisps of sunlight fled as the train entered the enveloping darkness of the tunnel. The one thing she regretted most of all—she longed to tell Raphaël her feelings had never changed. She loved him now and always would.

CHAPTER 12

In the blink of an eye, the train squealed to a halt at the Centrale Station in La Spezia. Sarah was relieved she wouldn't be required to direct anyone to the hospital and made no attempt to locate Tyler or Gemma in the crowd. She felt numb and withdrawn. Her so-called friends had betrayed her. She was well-rid of them, but their treachery hurt.

Sarah waited until everyone had exited the cabin. Then she stood wobbling somewhat and dragged her suitcase from the compartment and onto the platform below. She pushed loose tendrils of hair away from her face. With her head down, she bulldozed a path through passengers waiting to board. Then, she pulled her case upright and stopped in the station, needing time to think.

It was Tuesday. The original plans had been that she and Gemma would take the train tomorrow morning to Rome and spend their last day and a half exploring before flying home from Fiumicino Airport on

Thursday morning. But why hang around? There was no reason why she couldn't leave for Rome right away. She threw back her shoulders and decided. She would not let anything ruin her last two days in Italy. But she wasn't dragging her case any further than she had to.

It rumbled ominously behind her. A couple of the wheels were juddering dangerously. Ignoring them, she gritted her teeth and forged through the throngs of people milling about, their eyes trained on the overhead signs showing train times and track numbers. Hauling the infernal luggage out the main doors, she looked for a taxi. They weren't hard to spot, and she determinedly made her way to the closest one.

The short, heavyset man who drove it, leaned against the front fender, his lips sealed around the remains of a cigarette that he flicked to the sidewalk as she approached.

"*Serve un passaggio?*" he asked, stained teeth flashing an unusual shade of yellow in his darkly tanned face as he asked her if she needed a lift.

"*Si. Grazie,*" she responded with a sigh, drawing up before him and gladly relinquishing her luggage at long last. As he tossed it into the boot of his car she recited the address of her rooming house in perfect Italian. That much she was able to do well, as she'd had plenty of practise.

The driver nodded, sliding his bulk behind the wheel, and pulling precariously into traffic. Sarah stifled a yelp as a horn blared and a motorcyclist roared past them between two lanes of speeding traffic. She clung to the door handle vowing never to drive in Italy. But she admitted as they arrived outside her building, it did make for a fast trip.

Paying the man generously, Sarah stood on the sidewalk, staring at her room's window and considering her next move. It was still early. Yes, her heart felt as though it had shattered, but it wouldn't feel any better hanging around here.

She grasped the handle of her case and hauled it up the two crumbling steps to teeter on the landing while she entered the building's door code. Fortunately, since there were five floors to this tall, thin, rooming house, there was a tiny lift just inside the foyer. As the doors parted, Sarah stepped inside, the space just barely big enough for her and her luggage.

She dug out her keys. They jangled in her hand as she pushed a loose button with only the slight recollection of a three written upon its face. The ancient elevator wheezed into action. A pungent smell of garlic hung in the air as it had almost every day since she'd arrived. She smiled. The crusty old woman who ran the place, Lucia, was quite a character and would be missed.

The contraption shuddered to a halt and the doors only partially opened. Sarah pushed irritably at them, clearing enough space for her case to pass through. Lucia was in the hallway to her left with an equally old vacuum cleaner, humming to herself as she scrubbed it across a ratty looking carpet.

"*Ciao*, Sarah. *Parti oggi o domani?*" Lucia trod on the back end of the machine and its high-pitched howling ceased.

The little lady had never learned much English, but

Sarah knew enough Italian to deduce that Lucia wondered if she was leaving today or tomorrow.

"*Ciao*," she returned the greeting. "*Parto oggi.* I will leave today." She smiled at the little lady who hurried over to wrap Sarah in an embrace, kissing her soundly four times in rapid succession.

Lucia was, perhaps, even older than the building itself. Sun-wrinkled hands waved in the air as she spoke and her face was a leathery maze of lines surrounded by a froth of snow white hair. Her eyes, sunken deep within her olive complexion, looked to have seen it all; a thousand tales of wars, plagues, and pestilence, along with every injustice and horror known to man. But they also twinkled with kindness and good humour. There was always a smile on Lucia's face as she bustled about the building in her trademark flowered dresses, scuffed, sensible brown shoes, and thick hosiery that had long since given up any semblance of elastic. Even now it pooled about her ankles in heavy folds.

She kept the rented rooms scrupulously clean, but Sarah had seen Lucia's own personal space once. It was littered with stacks of newspapers, piles of clothes, and boxes of memorabilia, all of which smelled vaguely like garlic, onions, and tomato sauce, which somehow wasn't surprising.

"I wish you good," Lucia enunciated each English word, almost at a shout. Clearly, she believed if one said a thing loud enough it wouldn't matter what language was being spoken, the message would be received as intended.

"*Grazie di tutto.*" Sarah thanked the lady in Italian, hoping she'd gotten it right.

"*Buon viaggio,*" Lucia beamed. With a final pat to Sarah's arm, the little lady turned back to her work and Sarah felt strangely like crying. This shabby little place had been her home for the past two months and the little lady had mothered all who passed through her doors.

Sarah used the large key on her chain to open the door and step inside. The dark wood furniture that greeted her had been off-putting when she'd first arrived in June, but now she looked upon the bed, bureau, and substantial armoire as old friends. Also surrounding her was the familiar, faded wallpaper of yellow and brown leaves that made Sarah think of a warm fall day, the colourful patchwork quilt, and the red velvet curtains she'd grown to love. Well-worn floorboards creaked beneath her weight as she crossed to the bed. It wouldn't be easy to say goodbye to this temporary life she'd had, but it needed to be done.

Hoisting the suitcase onto the quilt, Sarah began re-rolling its contents to make room for more. She stripped off the cute outfit from this morning, feeling as if somehow she was purging her old acquaintances, and ground it into a crevice between her jeans and a pair of red flats she'd brought, but had never worn. Maybe she would now.

Pulling the shoes out, she chose a white sun dress sprinkled with red cherries to wear with them. The dress was one of her favorites. She often wore it when she needed cheering up and goodness knows that time was now.

The other clothes she'd worn while away, she stuffed in a mesh laundry bag to be washed when she got home.

The rest were shoved, without much regard for wrinkles, into the case. A second, smaller bag was retrieved from the corner armoire. When both suitcases were jammed full and zipped up, she slid them onto the floor and surveyed the room one last time. It was just as well she was leaving now. Best to make a clean break. She laid her set of keys on top of the bureau and swung around, tears blurring her vision as she groped for the door.

She couldn't hear Lucia vacuuming outside, and hoped she would be spared another goodbye. She didn't think she could hold herself in check much longer and didn't want to dissolve upon the poor woman in a fit of hysterics.

Stifling a sob, she poked her head into the hallway to ensure she was alone. Gemma's room was just to her right at the end of the hall, and four other young, Italian students stayed in rooms to the left. Sarah prayed she could escape without running into anyone else. Leaving this place she'd called home for two months felt like the culmination of her loss. She would have been sad to leave La Spezia regardless of what had happened in the Cinque Terre. But now, having lost Raphaël, the man she hadn't even known she wanted, her departure was made worse. Much worse.

She pulled the door closed and leaned against it. She was leaving behind the only man she'd ever loved, the one she'd once dared to dream might be hers. Again, Raphaël's face swam before her eyes. His eyes shone, filling her heart with joy at a mere glance, and his smile lighting her entire world.

Sarah took a deep shuddering breath. She could

almost smell the scent of his cologne fusing with the salty air of the sea in the moonlight. But, as it was with most visions, it was slipping away and vanishing like a dream upon waking. The back of her throat constricted until it became difficult to swallow.

Hot, unhappy tears pooled in her eyes, a bitter concoction of emotions that traced a fiery trail down her cheeks. She tasted them—salty and sad. Without listening closely, she could hear the sound of her heart breaking, the rhythm of her life ceasing to exist, the sound of her past, her hopes and dreams, her future—all dying within her.

Moving like an automaton, she draped her purse around her shoulders, and within each hand, dragged both shiny silver cases to the door of the elevator. Stopping, she reached for the button to open the doors, imagining it would be waiting for her, only to realise it was already in use, chugging up from far below. She dragged a hand across her eyes, unconcerned that it came away black with streaks of watery mascara. Whoever was coming would doubtlessly pass her by and she was past caring.

The elevator groaned and creaked as it climbed, a metal needle above the doors announcing its progress—second floor. She placed a hand on the wall, bracing herself as her head drooped, and she allowed the sobs to claim her. Her misery was complete.

The elevator shook and trembled as it rose—until it stopped. The doors skidded open partway and then jammed. She heard a muffled curse from within and flattened herself against the wall. Just her luck the person was getting off on her floor. She hiccupped and drew a sharp breath in hopes of stemming the tide of tears.

"Sarah?"

Oh no, the voice was known to her. She shook her head, blinking to clear her vision, but the figure swam in a sea of briny water. She struggled to make sense of what was happening.

"Sarah," the voice said again, with deepening sorrow, "my dear sweet girl. What have I done to you?" Arms slid around her sagging body, bearing her up and gathering her close. She resisted, thinking it a figment of her imagination and couldn't possibly be who she thought it was.

But through a haze, she saw warm brown eyes and a sparkle of tears within their depths. She saw his hair and the way he brushed it off his forehead. And his smile. Oh...Raphaël's smile melted her sorrow with the warmth of a blazing sun. His voice was smooth, rich, and beautiful.

She leaned back, sniffing the way he smelled like a clean day with salt from the ocean and then pressed herself to him, throwing her arms around his neck, the tears coming anew.

"You're here," she said in a strangled voice. "Why?"

"*D'abord*, to apologise." One hand splayed against the small of her back to hold her close while the other began a slow stroking of her hair. He rested his cheek against hers for a moment before pulling away to look at her. "Can you ever forgive me for the harshness I showed you?"

Sarah looked at him, becoming acutely aware of her disheveled state and tried again to wipe the tears from her face. His gaze dropped from her eyes to her cheeks, and he bent to kiss one tear away. Her heart caught in her throat at the tenderness of the action.

"Harshness?" she echoed blankly.

"Yes, my sweet." His hand went back to her hair, his eyes riveted on hers. "I thought you were promised to another man and were toying with me for a diversion. Enjoying a little 'oliday flirtation like the last time we met." His eyes clouded with pain. "When Tyler arrived, announcing that you were to be married, I was devastated."

"But it wasn't true," she said, her voice breaking. She cleared her throat and tried again. "I've never been engaged to Tyler...and I never loved Tyler. Gemma set the whole thing up in the Cinque Terre and used you as a pawn."

It was Raphaël's turn to look confused. "A...pawn? What is this thing?"

"It's a chess game piece, but what I mean is that she used you and me to further her own purpose. She wanted Tyler for herself, but he was determined to have me...I mean, my parents' money." There was so much to tell this fabulous man before her, but most important was her need to make him see the bottom line.

"But...you say you 'ave never loved this, Tyler?"

Sarah took his face between her hands and searched his worried brown eyes, feeling the rough stubble of his beard under her fingers. "I have *never* loved him," she repeated with emphasis.

"Then you are free to love someone else? Per'aps a Frenchman, about my size with a 'ungry look in 'is eye?" A slow smile was stretching across his handsome face.

"Because you can be assured, 'e loves you." Raphaël's eyes darkened with the intensity of his emotion.

"I already do," she murmured. "I always have, ever since we first met."

Lips met eagerly. Their joining was like the crack of a whip, the snapping of a breaking rope, or the thundering noise of a hurricane. Sarah tasted the sweetness of his mouth, inhaling deeply to fill her lungs with his scent. Their arms entwined, seeking to pull one another closer. A moan of pleasure escaped Raphaël's lips as their mouths connected, and their breathing quickened as they strove to make up for all the lost years.

CHAPTER 13

"It's what I always imagined it could be," Sarah whispered that same evening, half to herself. "But didn't ever think it was possible." She snuggled up to Raphaël on the steps of the fountain in Piazza di Santa Maria, staring up at the Basilica of Our Lady in the heart of Trastevere, a popular neighbourhood in Rome. He wrapped a protective arm around her and squeezed her close.

"You mean Roma?" he asked. Bending close, he kissed the top of her head.

"No, I mean sure..." She grinned up at him, thinking she could stay like this forever. "That too, I suppose, but actually, I was referring to us."

"Ahh. The love we share, *oui*?"

"*Oui*," she agreed. "I'm feeling quite grateful to Gemma at this moment. If it weren't for her and her meddling, we might never have found one another again." She stretched her legs out in front of her with a sigh of contentment.

"It is true. I cannot believe the lengths she went to though. Calling Angelina to learn which B&B was run by my friends, asking 'er when I would be there, and then booking rooms at the same time would 'ave taken a lot of work."

"Not to mention talking me into it and then somehow getting Tyler to join us." Sarah shook her head. "I still don't fully understand that."

"I do," Raphaël said with a shrug. "She 'oped to put us together and then surprise us in a compromising position with Tyler at 'er side. Then 'e would drop you, and she could play the part of a supportive friend, all in a romantic setting sure to make 'im fall for 'er. *Voila.*" He snapped his fingers.

Sarah laughed. "I think you're right. I'm just grateful Romeo looked back at the train station and saw me alone while the pair of them left together. Otherwise, you'd still be thinking Tyler and I were a couple."

"*Non, ma chérie.* They would 'ave returned and it would have been obvious, but..." he leaned over and gave her a lingering kiss, before he added, "It would 'ave been too late to stop you from leaving. I would 'ave 'ad to tear Rome apart to find you."

"I believe you would have." Sarah gasped as his mouth came down on hers, fierce with passion. Her heart flared in response, and they melted together for a long moment. A warm wind whirled through the piazza, lifting her hair to twine around their heads before she pulled away to press her blonde curls into submission.

"We should walk," she said breathlessly. "It's so pretty here." She jumped to her feet and turned to pull him up. They walked together, arm in arm. "And we should find you some clothes to wear tomorrow. You left your things behind in a rush," she teased.

"I 'ave all I need right 'ere," he said, looking into her eyes meaningfully.

Sarah flushed with happiness. Could this really be happening? One minute her world was crumbling around her ears, and the next she was deliriously happy. When Raphaël had told her he meant to go with her to Rome, she was thrilled. It was like living in a dream. One you hoped never to wake up from.

"But yes," he continued in resignation. "I should buy a few things such as a toothbrush, another set of clothes, and perhaps a brush." He ran fingers through his unruly mane of hair. "When one is in love, it is difficult to think of such mundane things."

They strolled along the ancient streets of Trastevere enjoying the glowing brick buildings in the last light of the day. The alleys were narrow, barely wide enough for two people, however, so picturesque that they took their time on the cobblestone road, each rock smoothed and rounded by centuries of wear and tear.

Rome was beautiful, and the evening stretched before them with possibility. The city was alive with the sounds of a culture that had existed for more than two thousand years. They fell silent, each wrapped in his or her contentment at just being together as the noise of the city whispered around them.

The soft tones of people singing, the bells in a church tower calling people for prayer, the steady hum of traffic, and a honking of motor scooters provided a melodious backdrop.

A gentle breeze smelled of coffee with the pungent

aroma of fresh food from the many restaurants that spilled onto the narrow lane. Sarah breathed deep, suddenly feeling hungry. Apart from a sandwich, bought from a vendor at the train station in La Spezia, she'd eaten nothing.

"I know the perfect place," Raphaël spoke as though reading her mind. "It is why I brought you to this spot, *ma chérie.*"

He led her down a street even narrower than the one before and Sarah saw white umbrellas set over tiny tables in front of a thriving restaurant. Twinkle lights glimmered over the doors and peeked through the boughs of a gnarled old tree that bowed low over the tables. Nearby walls hung heavy with vines, and assorted clay containers, filled with a variety of flowers, added charm.

A clatter of dishes emanated from within the cheerful interior and delicious smells wafted out to greet them. The outside space was a perfect extension of the inside, with tables draped in checkerboard cloths and candles just waiting to be lit. Sarah almost clapped her hands at the beauty of it.

Despite it being busy, they were seated right away. Raphaël helped her to translate the menu and order before he poured them each a cool glass of sparkling prosecco.

Smiling Raphaël leaned forward, his fingers wrapped around his glass as he held it out for a toast.

"*Santé,*" Sarah said. The glasses clinked together joyously.

"*À nous.*" Raphaël corrected with a nod. "To us." His brown eyes held hers in a look filled with promise.

Tempted to pinch herself, Sarah tipped her goblet and took a sip. The wine leapt on her tongue, and when she swallowed, the sweetness lingered in her mouth. Was it even legal to feel this happy, she wondered?

They each ordered a pizza. It had arrived, straight from the fire brick oven she could see through a window inside, sizzling on the plates set before them.

"I'm not sure I can eat all of this," she said doubtfully. But she did, and in record time. Replete, she sat back to breathe, but Raphaël wasn't finished. Calling to their server, he asked that two panna cottas be brought for dessert. Sarah couldn't protest, even though she was stuffed full already. As Sarah slid her spoon through the smooth, creamy dessert a few minutes later, and lifted it dripping with a ruby-red raspberry sauce to her mouth, she thought she'd died and gone to Heaven.

"Oh! That's absolutely fabulous," she exclaimed. "I've never had it before."

Raphaël beamed, clearly pleased with his choice.

When they had finished the plates had been removed by the server, and after much praise from Sarah for the chef, Raphaël suggested rather than sitting any longer, they should walk.

"It will be good for the digestion," he said, pulling out her chair. Sarah sensed there was more to it than that, but she was happy just to be with him. They fell into step together, hand in hand as she'd dreamt.

They spoke of the olive groves and vineyards on Raphaël's estate that he shared with his brother, Julien in Provence. They discussed Sarah's parents, winters in Canada, the time of her flight on Thursday, and finally, what she might do when she returned home. By this time, they had left Trastevere behind them and Raphaël led the way to *Ponte Sisto*, a pedestrian bridge spanning the Tiber River.

"Are you tired? Or shall we continue a little further?" he asked.

They had ridden the train for almost five hours that afternoon. Sarah was happy to be moving and exploring the ancient city of Rome. It was like an open-air museum of history and art. But they could have been walking through a field of cattle, and it wouldn't have made a difference to how Sarah enjoyed her surroundings. It was not the places they went, or the things they saw together, but the company with her.

SHE NODDED, KNOWING SHE WOULD FOLLOW HIM anywhere, but feeling that perhaps things were too new to put that sentiment into words. The moon rode high overhead, its light a little subdued thanks to all the streetlamps, but its presence felt nonetheless. It bathed them with a milky light as they descended the stone staircase next to the bridge and Raphaël took her hand in his once more. The cobblestones continued on a wide promenade created right beside the water.

She wasn't keen on responding to his question as to what she would do back in Canada. Maybe he'd drop it now they meandered beside the softly rippling waters of the Tiber River. She didn't want to think of returning home and leaving him behind again. It was a painful subject she wouldn't allow herself to dwell on.

They walked in silence for several minutes. The moon glimmered on the water, riding the swiftly flowing current, while streetlights illuminated cypress trees planted on the opposite bank. It was peaceful and quiet. The only sounds made were of their own footsteps on the smooth cobbles. Sarah rested her head on Raphaël's shoulder and he pulled her closer, leaving his arm around her waist as he guided them along.

"Shall we sit for a moment?" Raphaël asked. In answer, Sarah stopped and they settled themselves on the paved edge of the walkway. As she stared out across the expanse of water she thought of the thousands of years this river had made this very same journey and the countless people whose lives had depended on it.

"I asked you what you might do when you return to Canada?" he said, reminding her.

"I—I'd rather not talk about that, if you don't mind. I want to savour every moment with you tonight."

"I understand." He picked up a small pebble from the walkway and leaning back he hurled it out across the flowing river. "But...what if you didn't go back?" he said quietly.

"What if I...What do you mean?" Sarah's heart began to race, and her hands were instantly damp. She turned to look into his face.

"What if you stayed with me?" he said. "You could teach English in France just as well as you could in Italy." He spoke faster with each uttered word and wiped his hands down the front of his pant legs as though his too were clammy.

"You mean—live with you? On the estate? With Angelina and Julien? As your girlfriend?"

"No," he added quickly. "As my—my wife." In the twilight of a Roman night, he turned to her and clasped both her hands, bringing them to his lips to kiss each one in turn. His eyes glittered in the light of the moon. "I love you, Sarah. I 'ave loved you from the first moment I saw you so many years ago. There is no one for me but you." He paused to take a ragged breath. "I 'ave no ring to offer and no fine speech arranged. I was unprepared to see you and to fall in love all over again. I know this is sudden, but...I'm asking you to marry me. I would make you 'appy. We would 'ave a good life together, you and me. Will you think about it, *mon amour*?" His fingers stroked the soft flesh of her palms as he looked earnestly into her eyes.

The night air was warm, and the stars bright, glittering like diamonds in the velvety darkness of the indigo sky. She smiled. Sarah didn't need to think. She'd thought about Raphaël for the last five years. She looked into his eyes and saw all the colors of the world —bright sunsets, clear lakes, and blue skies. She felt cherished and desired and loved. There was no hesitation now. She knew in her soul that marrying this man would be like coming home.

"Yes, Raphaël...yes I will marry you. I love you." Sarah laughed and threw her arms around his neck. He pulled her close and buried his face in her hair. The moonlight glided over the water beside them, bathing them in its radiance.

CHAPTER 14

The whitewashed church appeared before her, its uppermost points draped in gold, making Sarah think of a crown. The impressive building was like a beacon, gleaming in the light of day, drawing guests and family members alike as witnesses to the union of their blissful day.

Her limousine drew to a halt, and a well-dressed man hurried down the steps to open Sarah's door. She gathered her train in one hand and delicately stepped from the car, her long, white, strapless gown clinging to every curve before cascading in silken folds from her knees to the toes of her satin pumps. Her hair had been arranged into a low chignon at the nape of her neck, the golden curls embellished with pearl and crystal hairpins. She felt beautiful, knowing joy had lent her an added beauty today. How could it not? Soon, she would be wed to the man of her dreams.

Sarah lifted a bouquet of white roses to her nose and drank in the sweet scent as she waited for her parents to exit the vehicle and join her. They hugged, then Sarah linked arms with her father on one side and her mother on the other. Gathering her skirt in the other hand, they ascended the steps, their heels clicking on the stone. Her dress whispered around her legs as they reached the entrance to the church and swept into the foyer, knowing Raphaël waited for her inside.

Angelina hurried forward to wrap Sarah in her arms, tears bright in her eyes. She wore a long, form-fitting dress in the ruby-red colour that suited her dark hair so well. Sarah and she had chosen it on one of their many excursions. They'd spent endless hours together, planning for an October wedding once Sarah and Raphaël had arrived at the chateau with their exciting news.

Gabrielle was there as well, clad in a similar red gown. Alone, she had flown in this morning from Paris to be the second bridesmaid.

"I'm so very 'appy for you both," she said in her beautiful French accent. "Welcome to the family." She kissed Sarah's cheeks four times and then clasped her close. Stepping back, she sniffed and blinked rapidly.

Four-year-old Celeste was the flower girl and shyly peeped at Sarah from behind her mother's skirts in a frilly dress created with layers of white tulle embossed with red roses.

"Come here sweetie." Sarah bent down and held out her arms. The little girl pattered toward her in tiny, patent leather shoes.

"Celeste, you are so pretty today, and just look at those shoes," Sarah said admiringly. The little girl nodded proudly as she stuck out a foot to regard her footwear with pleasure. She held a basket filled with red and white rose petals that tipped precariously, spilling a few onto the wooden floor.

"Careful," admonished her mother, Angelina, although she looked on indulgently as Sarah held the child close. Sarah straightened. The two women had prepared for this special day at the chateau together that morning. Though Angelina had arrived at the church even earlier since Julien was Raphaël's best man.

"Ready?" Sarah's father, Allan asked. He was tall and distinguished in a charcoal grey suit and button down with red tie. His thinning hair had been trimmed neatly and a red rose had been threaded into his lapel. He turned to his wife and motioned her forward. "Honey," he said urgently, "you should go with the usher to be seated now."

Sarah reached out to her mother, Esther, who stood dabbing at her eyes with a tissue a few paces back.

Esther was a youthful woman, who could pass for Sarah's older sister, or so everyone said. Her blue eyes and blonde hair, just like her daughter's locks, had been cut into a long bob. Although a few greys had begun to appear of late. She was slim and stylish, wearing a fitted sheath in muted tones of gold and cream. With a shuddering sigh, she stepped forward now to clasp Sarah's hand.

"I'm not sure I can do this without crying," she declared, dabbing yet again.

"You'll be fine. But I want you to stay and walk with me, one on either side. Please?" Sarah squeezed her mother's hand. The lady nodded, taking a deep breath and tucking the tissue into her matching clutch.

"I love you honey," she said with a wobbly smile.

The three of them stood behind Angelina near the main entrance.

Faint strains of music could be heard inside. The double doors into the sanctuary were suddenly flung open by two men in dark suits who nodded decorously at the little group. Angelina straightened the white basket in Celeste's chubby hand and sent her off down the aisle as the congregation stood to watch the procession.

Celeste lost all stage fright as she stepped daintily along, tossing petals in front, to either side, and, to everyone's delight, a few over her shoulders in front of Gabrielle. A ripple of laughter ran through the assembly. Angelina, with a wink of one eye, left Sarah in the foyer as she too walked slowly down the aisle behind Gabrielle.

Then, it was Sarah's turn. Her heartbeat increased as she stepped forward, flanked by her parents. The delicate white fabric of her dress billowed around her with each step, carrying her away from the past and into the future she and Raphaël imagined together.

She saw dear Elyse, Raphaël's mother, dabbing at tears of joy in a bright dress of green silk, and her husband Armand, close beside her in his charcoal grey suit nodding happily. Dark-haired Philippe sat quietly on the church pew between them, content to stuff his little mouth with crackers from a box on his lap. Dressed in a miniature suit like his father's, he looked every inch the cherub that he was, with plump, rosy cheeks stuffed to capacity.

. . .

Luna waved from a spot partway along the aisle too. She had worn something less splashy than her usual wild sundresses, as she had donned a simple grey dress with muted pink roses and matching rose-coloured pumps. Romeo stood at the front of the church beside Julian, both men standing up for Raphaël in black tuxedoes. They both looked quite debonair with their dark hair slicked back and big grins on their faces. Sarah smiled and nodded at each one.

Raphaël was resplendent in a black tuxedo with a white rose tucked into his collar. His black hair was pushed away from his dark eyes that regarded her with love as she walked toward him down the aisle.

The ivory-colored floor of the chapel glowed beneath her feet. Sunlight streaming in through the tall windows bathed the room in a golden light. Each step took her closer to Raphaël, and Sarah could feel her heart sing with anticipation. This was the moment she had dreamed of since Raphaël had proposed to her in Rome. Her smile was brighter than the shafts of sunlight arching through the stained glass windows beside her as she walked down the aisle to meet her true love.

. . .

The air was thick with the heady scent of dozens of roses, their aroma intoxicating. They filled every inch of the church along with the glad expectations of the assembled crowd. Guests, including Angelina's parents who had flown from Canada; Lia, Raphaël's sister and her husband Mathéo, and their children Maxine and Marcel—all radiated happiness. They had been waiting for this moment and sat in hushed reverence as the bride and groom prepared to pledge their love.

As the music softly played, Raphaël held out his hands, and Sarah placed hers within them. He lightly kissed her knuckles before giving her an adoring smile. His eyes met hers, and in them she saw all the promises he had made, and all the wonderful dreams they had dreamed together.

The priest stepped forward to begin the ceremony, but before he spoke, Raphaël whispered something into the bride's ear.

"I 'ave waited a lifetime for this moment, *mon amour*."

The priest began the ceremony with scripture, and the two exchanged rings with vows—their words spilling into the air and taking hold in the hearts of those gathered. As they kissed, the guests erupted into cheers, and in a moment of pure joy their love was sealed.

But before they turned to greet the world as husband and wife, Raphaël moved to take the white rose from his lapel. He handed it to the bride. On its petals, he had inscribed a single word, 'Love.' Sarah thought her heart would burst.

As they strode down the aisle arm in arm, Raphaël said, "We have fulfilled our destiny, my love. You and I were meant to be together." He stole another kiss and added, "The future is ours."

The sun shone upon them as they stepped outside to thank their guests and make their way to the waiting car. As they drove into the sunset with the rose still in her hands, Sarah and Raphaël waved to their guests, their hearts singing the melody of a happy future. Destiny had brought them together, and love would keep them.

EPILOGUE

Sarah checked the time, then placed her phone on the bedside table and slid beneath the cozy comforter to snuggle up to Raphaël once more. Lifting an arm, he pulled her close and nuzzled her hair. The morning sounds of faraway traffic and early rising cicadas crept through the open windows of the Chateau Belliveau where they had an entire wing to themselves. The April breeze that drifted over them was warm, even though it wasn't quite seven in the morning.

Heavy mahogany furniture was placed strategically about the enormous bedroom, but the dove grey walls and creamy white floor tiles softened the space. A chandelier tinkled ever so slightly in the breeze at the center of the room, casting a glittering kaleidoscope of dancing lights during the evening hours.

"I forgot to tell you something last night." Sarah straightened the thin strap of her white lace nightgown on her shoulder and placed a kiss on his bare chest. "This weekend, Angelina and I are thinking of flying to

Paris. Is that alright with you, my love?" She tilted her head back to look into his face.

"Is it Gabrielle?" he asked, a frown appearing on his forehead.

"Yes. She's having a hard time over the sudden breakup. Lyam appears to have disappeared into thin air. Gabrielle hasn't said much about the reasons for it but we know she's hurting. Anyway, we think she needs the support of her family. Annette will meet us there."

Raphaël smiled. "You care so much. *Merci mon amour*." He dropped a light kiss on the end of her nose. "Gabrielle will be glad to see 'er sister and, of course, you and Angelina, 'er two adopted cousins. But you will only 'ave to leave again, and she will be alone. Per'aps she should come 'ome for a while."

"She's determined to finish her degree. It's so close to completion." Sarah came up on her elbow and traced an idle finger across his chest. "We want to surprise her and try to jolt her out of the depressing way she's been talking. Besides, it'll do us all good to be together."

"*D'accord*, I agree," he said, capturing her hand and bringing it to his lips. "I can manage without you for a few days, I suppose."

"Only two," she grinned at him. "I have to get back for school on Monday."

"Of course. I am so proud of what you 'ave accomplished with your students and of 'ow your French 'as improved."

"*Merci beaucoup, monsieur Belliveau*." Playfully she came up on all fours and kissed him. "I've had an excellent teacher. However, lovely as it would be to simply relax in bed with you all day, I think we should get up."

"Must we?"

Raphaël reached for her as she nimbly scrambled out of reach with a screech. Laughing, she landed on her feet and scampered into the bathroom, knowing if he caught her another hour would disappear. She had to get to the school for work.

Her job was fulfilling and she'd been lucky to get it. It wasn't full-time employment, of course. She didn't have a strong enough grasp of the French language to warrant it, but teaching a few classes of English each day was important to her.

Angelina was busy with Celeste, thrilled to be pregnant again and helping on the estate in other ways. Julien and Raphaël ran the family business producing olive oil and wine, or *vin rosé* as she'd come to know it. While Elyse and Armand spent most of their time travelling and living at his apartment in Nice. Everyone had a place in the family, and each contributed to the happiness of the whole.

As she brushed her teeth, readying for the day, she thought of Gemma and Tyler. She hadn't seen either of them since that fateful day in the Cinque Terre and was glad for it. Gemma had written a letter of contrition, well sort of. She'd apologised for the deception and betrayal. Only she'd ended it by blaming Sarah that she and Tyler were still not together. They were two 'friends' that Sarah didn't need in her life.

Which brought her to Gabrielle. She'd formed a close friendship with the younger woman that was built on mutual respect, trust, and love. She was family after all, but even if she hadn't been, Sarah would still have loved her.

She was concerned for the girl. Her last text had sounded so bleak. That was when Annette, Angelina, and Sarah had concocted a plan to visit her in Paris. They would do their best to cheer her, or at the very least check on her health. Gabrielle was pushing herself even harder now that Lyam had left her as he had.

Although Gabrielle had not explained the breakup, Sarah had a feeling there was more to it than just a simple parting of the ways. She knew, from something Gabrielle had let slip during a phone call, that the police had been involved.

Sarah sighed with worry as she pulled a brush through her glossy mane of curly blonde hair. If a weekend in Paris with the girls didn't snap Gabrielle out of her doldrums, she would see what else could be done.

Coming back into the bedroom, Sarah threw her brush on her dressing table. She walked over to her husband who stood at the floor length window, one hand pulling aside the filmy, cream-coloured curtains.

She stopped beside him to stare out at the fields of grape vines just waking from their winter nap. Taking a deep breath of fresh air, she rested her head on his chest, feeling perfectly happy. *Sometimes, dreams do come true.*

"It's going to be a beautiful day," she said, smiling into the face of the man she loved.

"It's going to be a beautiful life," he said, sliding an arm around her waist and holding her close.

If you enjoyed this book, it would mean so very much to me if you would leave a review. Thank you!

*READY FOR MORE ROMANCE? GET **WHEN LOVE BLOOMS IN PARIS**.*

JOIN MY MONTHLY NEWSLETTER FOR ALL THE LATEST news.

JOIN MY NEWSLETTER

Interested in hearing more about my books and upcoming releases? Be sure to sign up for my newsletter at **https://helentoews.com/newsletter** *so you don't miss a beat.*

ABOUT THE AUTHOR

I'm an author, humorist, work in education, and carry a license to drive anything on wheels (stilettoes and lipstick optional). I grew up and still reside on the family farm near Marshall, Saskatchewan, Canada. We raise Charolais cattle and gophers (the latter being purely coincidental). While the countryside is dear to my heart, my passion is to travel.

Among other things, I write sweet, destination romance.

Each book is set in an exotic destination we all would love to visit, allowing my readers an opportunity to escape to a fabulous region of Europe. There are twists and turns along the way that will keep you guessing, but always a happy ending.

Printed in Great Britain
by Amazon